"It took two
   to get into

He was moving away from her as he spoke. "And it's going to take two of us to get out of it. If you want to know the chances of a fast divorce, you come right along with me to the United States." He drained the contents of his drink before turning back to look at her. "Nothing to say?"

"Would it make any difference?"

"No."

"Then I'm not going to waste my breath," Sara said, her voice rough. "But if I do go to Nevada I'll be traveling separately and staying separately."

"You'll be going my way, or no way at all." Dave was standing back, his eyes steely.

A pulse jerked suddenly at her temple. There was to be no further discussion on the subject. The decision was to be entirely hers.

KAY THORPE, an English author, has always been able to spin a good yarn. In fact, her teachers said she was the best storyteller in the school—particulary with excuses for being late! Kay then explored a few unsatisfactory career paths before giving rein to her imagination and hitting the jackpot with her first romance novel. After a roundabout route, she'd found her niche at last. The author is married with one son.

Books by Kay Thorpe

These books may be available at your local bookseller.

Don't miss any of our special offers. Write to us at the following address for information on our newest releases.

Harlequin Reader Service
901 Fuhrmann Blvd., P.O. Box 1397, Buffalo, NY 14240
Canadian address: P.O. Box 603,
Fort Erie, Ont. L2A 9Z9

KAY THORPE

win or lose

Harlequin Books

TORONTO • NEW YORK • LONDON
AMSTERDAM • PARIS • SYDNEY • HAMBURG
STOCKHOLM • ATHENS • TOKYO • MILAN

Harlequin Presents first edition December 1986
ISBN 0-373-10941-5

Original hardcover edition published in 1986
by Mills & Boon Limited

CHAPTER ONE

SPREAD across two full columns of the back page, the photograph itself would have stood out regardless of subject. From where she sat on the opposite seat of the carriage, Sara read the headline over it:

DAVE LYNESS REGAINS WORLD CHAMPIONSHIP

The news had been out since the early hours, of course, but it still made impact. Everyone responded to a comeback. The new champion himself had entered into the spirit of the moment with a triumphant lofting of the silver cup. Only the cynic might read irony into that smile of his. Today he was news, next week it would be back to the small print. Fame made a fickle mistress.

Eyes lifted from their perusal of the newspaper, drawn perhaps by the instinctive feeling of being under surveillance. Sara smiled at the young man.

'I was looking at the sports columns,' she acknowledged. 'Sorry if I disturbed you.'

'You didn't,' he hastened to deny, returning the smile. 'Would you like to borrow it?'

Sara shook her head. 'There's no need, thanks.'

'Which sport are you interested in?' he insisted, turning to the rear page.

Her shrug was light. 'More a passing curiosity. Snooker isn't really my game.'

'Mine neither when it comes to playing, though I always watch the televised matches when I can.' He tapped the page in front of him with a forefinger. 'Saw this last night. Great finish! Didn't think Lyness was

5

going to make it after being eight down earlier. Second time in three years. Not bad considering he was twenty-nine before he turned professional. Going to have his work cut out to hang on to it though, with all the young talent in the game.' A rueful smile touched his lips as he caught her eye. 'Sorry, I'm going on a bit. Travelling through to Leeds?'

'No,' Sara responded. 'Sheffield.'

'Business trip?'

'No,' she said again. 'Personal.'

He took the hint, though without embarrassment, glance openly appraising as it rested on her face within its frame of softly layered dark hair. Blue eyes looked right back at him, a certain amusement in their depths. He was probably a couple of years younger than her own twenty-five, she reflected, but confident to a degree. Midlands, judging from his accent.

There was a click overhead followed by the hollow, echoing voice of the guard announcing the approach to Derby station.

'I get out here,' stated Sara's carriage companion. 'Pity,' he added regretfully.

'Yes, isn't it.' With the stop coming up any moment she could afford to be generous. 'Nice having someone to chat with on a journey.'

Coming to his feet as the train slowed, he took down the holdall from the overhead rack and rested it on the seat while he drew on a lightweight anorak. Cords, not jeans, she noted idly, but almost definitely a student. Returning from the Easter break, perhaps?

'Might as well have this,' he said, dropping the newspaper in her lap as he left the carriage. 'Save carrying it. Sheffield's next but one stop, by the way,' he added from the doorway.

'Thanks.' Sara lifted a hand in casual farewell. ''Bye.'

They were moving again before she picked up the

paper, turning to the back page to study the photograph. Tall, and leanly built in his black waistcoat and trousers, Dave Lyness seemed to be gazing right into her eyes. A hardboned face, skin tautly stretched, his crisply styled hair gleaming with health and vitality in the flashlight. The total, indisputable male; king of a world still run largely for and by the male. There were women who played snooker, even ladies' championships, but if the day ever came when both sexes would compete on the same level it wouldn't be yet awhile. Not while men like this one had any say in the matter.

She drifted a little over the following half-hour, coming back to earth with a jerk when Chesterfield was announced. Another fifteen minutes and she would be at journey's end—this particular part of it at any rate. Exactly how she was going to handle matters when she did reach her final destination she wasn't yet sure. It didn't do to plan too far ahead. Things had a way of going wrong. Better to play it by ear, to take it as it came, to cross her bridges when she reached them—whichever cliché best fitted. Twenty-four hours from now, with any luck, she would be back home in London with a chance of setting her life to rights again in the not-too-distant future. That had to be worth any effort.

Late afternoon sunlight welcomed her emergence from the vaulted entrance hall of the station. Swinging her overnight case easily in one hand, she turned right to the taxi rank, relieved to find there was no queue of people waiting in line. She gave the first driver the address and got into the back, settling into the seat as he started the engine. Making allowances for the traffic at this hour of the day, it was going to take at least twenty minutes to get where she was going. Long enough to relax and compose herself for what was to come.

'Come in on the London train, did you?' asked the man up front without turning his head, as he joined the main road and headed left for the traffic island. 'What's the weather like down there?'

'About the same,' Sara acknowledged. 'Maybe a little warmer.'

'Always is,' came the cheerful response. 'Can't grumble, though. Been a good fortnight. Got the cup back again, did our Dave!'

He was obviously taking it for granted that she would know what he was talking about. Sara didn't disillusion him. 'I imagine you've been busy,' she said.

'Not half! Had more folk here this year than ever. It's going to seem real quiet now it's all over for another year. Pity we don't have more like it. What this place needs . . .'

He continued to expound on the subject of what Sheffield needed as a city while Sara listened with half an ear, putting in the occasional yes or no when it seemed called for, eyes on the passing scene. She felt churned up inside—almost ready to turn tail and retreat. Except that she had to go through with it. Having come this far there was no going back.

Her destination lay in the south-west suburbs of the town, situated at the end of a short cul-de-sac lined either side with large old houses built of weathered stone. Sara added a substantial tip when paying off her driver. He had probably kept her from brooding too deeply. She looked to the upper windows of the house before her as the taxi turned in a tight circle and moved off, but there was no sign of movement. Perhaps it hadn't been such a good idea to arrive without warning? Yet a letter had been beyond her, a phone call out of the question. Face to face, that was the only way.

The main door was closed and locked. Sara fished out her key ring and inserted one of the two Yale keys, half expecting to feel resistance; not altogether relieved when there was none. A further door to the left gave access to the lower of the two flats, but it was towards the red-carpeted staircase at the end of the bright hallway that she made, mounting quietly and pausing for a brief moment at the top, gathering her resources before crossing the landing. There was no answer to her knock. Nor to a second and slightly louder assault. She hoped the people in the lower flat were out too. Otherwise someone might be coming up to find out what unauthorised person had managed to get into the building.

Her second key fitted too, and once inside she felt at least temporarily secure. Dropping her case on the floor of the small lobby, she went on through to the living-room with its big bay window that looked out over trees still coming into full leaf to the suburban sprawl climbing one of the seven hills on which the city was built. Like Rome, someone had once half-jokingly remarked in her hearing. Anything less like Rome she had yet to find. It couldn't even truly be called Steel City any more because so much of the industry had disappeared; just another provincial centre lacking in almost everything that made life worthwhile—in her estimation, at least. But then she was prejudiced, she supposed. The London scene just happened to suit her style better.

The room was as she remembered it, the furnishings comfortable and well kept, the décor restrained. Heavy velvet curtains in a deep-blue colour graced the window, complementing the paler blue of the carpet and warmed by the soft sheen of leather, the glow of old mahogany. Sara slipped off the jacket of her grey wool suit and draped it across a chair arm before going through to the adjoining, sunlit kitchen. Filling the kettle at the sink, she plugged it in, then got down a cup and saucer from the cupboard above, together with a plate. If she was going to have a long wait she might just as well make herself comfortable. All she had had for lunch was coffee and a sandwich.

There were eggs in the refrigerator rack, and ham in the box. She plumped for scrambled eggs on toast. With that inside her and a cup of coffee in her hand, she felt better equipped to face what was coming. The only question was when?

Too restless to settle after she had drunk the coffee, she took a walk through the other rooms. The bathroom had a new suite, low slung and sumptuous in rich cream, the walls freshly tiled in copper brown. Even the towels toned into the scheme. An improvement without a doubt, but not exactly what she might have anticipated. A woman's touch, perhaps? A woman's suggestion, for sure. A thought that left a bitter taste in her mouth.

Like the living-room, the bedroom remained unaltered. There was the same beige carpet on the floor, the same brown and gold patterned duvet flung carelessly across the bed. In here the space was reduced by the built-in wardrobes and dressing-unit stretching across one whole wall, but it still left enough spare to make two of her bedroom back home. A modern flat bore no comparison unless one paid some fantastic price, that much she had to allow.

It was already approaching seven o'clock. She would wait until eight but no longer. There was always tomorrow, although the idea of spending a night contemplating it was far from attractive.

Going back to the living-room, Sara settled down in a chair with a copy of Graham Greene's *The Heart of The Matter*, chosen from a bookcase full for the most part of paperbacks. Her own influence here, though not exactly appreciated. From the pristine look of the cover, the book had never even been opened, much less read. No point in feeling slighted by the knowledge; the gesture itself had been a futile exercise. One more hour and then she would call a taxi and go and claim the hotel room already booked. Perhaps she might leave a note saying where she could be found. It would at least break the ice.

The room was dim when she opened her eyes. For a moment she was totally disorientated, her mind fogged by sleep. It took the sound of a key in the outer lock to bring her fully awake. She didn't rise, just sat there gazing at the lobby door as it opened to admit a tall, dark-suited figure. A couple of lamps sprang into life as a switch was depressed. Sara was the first to break the weighty silence.

'Hallo, Dave,' she said steadily.

Typically, he wasted no time on asking useless questions such as how she had got into the flat or how long she had been here. The first had to be obvious, the second immaterial. He closed the door again before speaking at all, face as expressionless as only he could make it.

'Why now?' he asked. 'It's been nearly two years.'

'That applies to both sides,' she pointed out. 'You never once attempted to contact me.'

'Persuade you, you mean?' Supple shoulders moved in a brief shrug. 'You made things clear enough at the time.'

'And no *real* man runs after a woman in your book, of course!' Her tone was quiet but barbed. 'That was half the problem with us, Dave.'

'If you say so.' He sounded indifferent. 'I'm going to make some coffee. Do you want any?'

'Why not?' She followed him to the kitchen, leaning on the door-jamb as he switched on the kettle and spooned brown powder from a jar into two mugs, ignoring the percolator she had used earlier. 'You still prefer instant, I see,' she commented on what was meant to be a light note, but came out sounding caustic instead.

'I'm not out to impress anybody,' he returned. 'All I need is the stimulant.'

'Alcohol is even quicker.'

'Except that I'm not in the mood.'

'Too much celebrating last night, perhaps?'

'Could be.' He glanced her way, face taut. 'Don't needle me, Sara. I've been in an Association meeting most of the day and I'm tired. The last thing I expected was to find you here.'

The last thing he wanted either, she assumed from his tone, and felt something contract deep down inside her.

'Don't you want to know why I'm here?' she asked.

'When you're ready to tell me.' He poured hot water into both mugs, added milk to one of them and held out the other to her. 'Maybe we'd better sit down.'

She moved ahead of him back into the other room and took her former seat, too tensed up inside to relax. Dave shed both jacket and tie, tossing them across the back of the sofa and sitting down to sling one ankle across the other knee in the casual manner she remembered so well. His hair was the colour of rich dark teak in the lamplight. Green eyes revealed little of what he was thinking.

'So shoot,' he invited. 'I don't imagine this was any social call.'

Sara took a slow deep breath. 'I want a divorce.'

Just for a moment the muscles around his mouth stiffened, although he made no movement. He even took a drink from the mug before responding to the bald statement.

'As simple as that?'

'You were always the one who liked things laid on the line,' she came back defensively, and saw his lip curl.

'You knew me all of six weeks. That can't be the only thing you remember.'

She said softly, 'I remember all of it, Dave. Every soul-destroying minute!'

His laugh came short and harsh. 'Still as quick to put the knife in! I should have been ready for that. If it's co-operation you're after, maybe you should try soft-pedalling for a change.'

Sara bit her lip. He had a point there. Getting across him wasn't going to help anything. 'It isn't going to be easy,' she said, and let the ambiguity of that statement stand for a deliberate moment before adding, 'Apparently, we need to be married three years before any application can be made, unless there are special circumstances.'

'Such as?'

She shrugged. 'Nothing that really applies to us.'

'Maybe I should have knocked you about a bit. That might have helped.' His tone was sardonic. 'It's still not too late if you're so desperate to be rid of me.'

'There are other ways.' She refused to rise to the taunt. 'We were married in America, we can get a divorce in America. It would be faster, and a lot less trouble.'

His eyes were on her face, cold and cynical. 'You've got it all worked out, haven't you?'

'As far as I'm able.' Sara felt oddly detached, as if she were observing the scene from somewhere outside herself even as her voice spoke the words. 'It took two of us to make the mistake, it's going to take two of us to unmake it. Uncontested, we might both have our freedom in a matter of weeks.'

'What makes you think I'll be going back to the States?'

'As the new world champion, you'll be playing at Lake Tahoe next month.' She gave him a bland little smile. 'Not exactly a journalistic scoop. They outbid

Vegas last year too.'

His expression hadn't altered. 'Are you proposing to come with me?'

'I'm suggesting you should go into it while you're over there,' she said. 'There's no use my going until there's some certainty that it can be arranged.'

'You mean your sources aren't all that reliable?'

'Let's just say they're not infallible.'

'Supposing it did work out,' he said after a moment. 'An American divorce might not even be valid over here.'

'If the marriage was there's every reason to suppose the divorce would be too. The point is, it's worth a try.'

Dave drained the mug and deposited it on the glass-topped table at his elbow before getting to his feet to cross over to the window. Hands thrust into trouser pockets, he stood there for a while gazing out at the twinkling lights across the park. Sara watched him, eyes following the lines of his lean, muscular body: back tapering down from shoulder to waist, to narrow hip and hard male buttock. She had followed those same lines with her hands on many occasions in the past, tracing out nerve paths, lingering to caress the long scar he carried across the top of one taut thigh. A motor-cycling accident when he was in his teens, she had learned. There was another under his hairline where he had narrowly escaped a fractured skull. No helmet, he had admitted. It hadn't even been his motor-cycle but one he had borrowed without permission; euphemism for stealing, he'd added with wry humour. At least, that was how the courts had looked on it. Injuries taken into account, he'd been lucky to escape with probation.

'Where were you planning on staying tonight?' he asked, bringing her back to the present.

'I'm booked at the Hallam,' Sara admitted. 'I told

them I'd be late checking in.'

He turned to look at her, eyes enigmatic. 'You could have said all you had to say over the phone, or by letter. Why take the trouble to come all this way for half-an-hour's chat?'

'I thought I owed you that much effort,' she said. 'Don't you?'

'Depends how you look at it. We've been apart ten times as long as we were together. Not much effort on view there.'

'From either side!' she flashed, and saw him smile humourlessly.

'Seems to be about where we came in. Relying on me taking you up there?'

Her chin jutted a fraction. 'I can always phone for a taxi.'

'The phone's out of order. I reported it this morning, but it could be a couple of days before they catch up on it.' He held up a hand mockingly as her expression altered. 'Don't worry, I don't expect you to stay here. There's still only the one bedroom, and I'm sure as hell not sleeping on the settee. We can talk in the morning. I've got a free day.'

'I need to be back in London by early evening,' she put in swiftly.

'So? If you leave after lunch you'll still make it.'

She hesitated before saying it. 'You haven't asked me why I want the divorce.'

'I said we'll talk about it in the morning. Right now I'm in no fit state to talk about anything rationally.' He was moving as he spoke, sliding into his jacket again but leaving the tie where it was. 'Is that case out there the only luggage you brought?'

'Apart from my handbag.' Sara went to get her own jacket, fastening the buttons with meticulous care. It was almost ten o'clock. She must have slept for a couple of hours at least; two late nights over the weekend hadn't helped. A good night's rest would see them both in better shape. Delaying her departure a few hours wasn't going to hurt anything.

Dave carried her case downstairs, following her out into fresh cool air and latching the door behind him. A silver blue XJS was parked across the gateway. Dave unlocked the nearside door and stuck the case down between front seat and back before standing aside to allow Sara to slide on to the soft leather.

'Nice,' she commented appreciatively as he came round to get behind the wheel. 'When did you get this?'

'I treated myself after I broke maximum in the Jameson. It left plenty of change.'

'I daresay it would.' She shook her head. 'It always leaves me bemused to realise just how much money there is to be made in professional snooker.'

'It wasn't always the same,' he said, starting the engine. 'Television and the world championships made it a supersport—but you know all that already. You should. If you hadn't been so all-fired eager for an inside look, we'd never have got together in the first place.'

He was right in that respect, Sara was bound to concede. Her journalistic instinct was wholly to blame. Too late now for regrets, she thought. Two whole years too late.

At this hour the streets were quiet. It took them little more than five minutes to reach the hotel. Dave drew up just short of the main doors, making no immediate attempt to get out of the car.

'About tomorrow,' he said. 'I'll call for you around eleven. We can drive out somewhere for lunch. There's a train around three that will get you in for five-thirty. That suit?'

'Just about.' She turned her head sideways a little to look at him, catching him profile-on against the light from the drive lamp beyond and feeling her stomach muscles respond. He still attracted her; he probably always would. The physical pull was a thing apart. His hands resting on the wheel were long-fingered and supple, capable of so many clever tricks. She remembered the feel of them on her body, knowledge-able, exciting, sometimes tender, sometimes almost brutal. A man of many moods, and few of them what one might expect. She added deliberately, 'Aren't you at least going to see me safely inside?'

'I might be recognised,' he said matter-of-factly. 'If you're with me, so might you. I don't expect you booked in under my name.'

Sara flushed, but kept her voice steady enough. 'How right you are—but then you always were!' She opened her door with a force that rocked it back on the stops. 'Don't bother getting my case out, I can manage!'

'I know,' he returned, unmoved, 'you always could. Be out here at eleven. I'll make sure I'm on time. Sleep tight, Sara.'

He passed her as she moved to the main doors, turning the car around the circle and driving off with a lift of one hand. There were plenty of people still around in the lobby, some of them in evening dress. The spillover from some function or other, Sara surmised. She checked in at the desk, received her room-key and tariff card, and made her way across to the lifts. Nothing about tonight had gone as she had planned. Her own fault, of course, for choosing to do it this way. She wasn't even sure now exactly what she *had* anticipated. Dave hadn't altered one iota. He never would alter.

Her room was on the third floor, much like any other hotel room in any reasonably good hotel, the accompanying bathroom small but well kept. Sara lost no time in stripping off the clothes she had worn for so many hours and stepping under a warm shower, soaping away the day's fatigue. It was too late to start thinking about a meal, but she could at least order something through room service, if it was only a sandwich. No coffee: she didn't want to be kept awake. Sleep held forgetfulness. It was what she needed most right now.

Briefly she contemplated telephoning Nigel, then decided against it. There would be time enough later when everything was settled, to confess the real purpose of her journey north. They could have waited out the three years if this posting hadn't come up. Come September, she had to be free to go with him. She wanted it as much as he did. Sir Nigel and Lady Rotherby: it would be a feather in her mother's cap if not in her own. For a man to gain a knighthood at forty-eight was achievement enough, only Nigel wasn't one to rest on his laurels. She wasn't in love with him, but she respected him more than any other man she had ever known, and that meant more. Love was at best a transient affair. She, of all people, knew that.

Room service proved to be surprisingly quick. By ten minutes past eleven she was ready to retire. Switching out the bedside light, she went to open the curtains, pausing for a moment or two to look out over the panoramic view of the twinkling city streets. By day there might be flaws visible; by night, with the air clear and the sky overhead spangled with stars, it was another place. Dave had travelled the world but he wouldn't live anywhere else. That had been another nail in the coffin of their relationship.

Sliding between the sheets, she tried to compose herself for sleep but her mind refused to switch off to order. Stray thoughts came together and fused, forming images which wouldn't dissolve. There was nothing to be gained from remembering, only she couldn't stop herself. Eventually she gave up the unequal struggle and went with the stream, right back to the very beginning, the night it had all started . . .

CHAPTER TWO

THE auditorium was hushed, all attention concentrated on the man poised above the tautly stretched green baize. Sighting along the cue, he looked perfectly relaxed—almost nonchalant. A concerted sigh went up as the blue cut back at a seemingly impossible angle to drop into the corner pocket, leaving the cue ball to come off the cushion into nigh on perfect position behind the pink. Only as the player straightened did the tension of the moment become evidenced in the faint movement of his lips as if releasing his own pent breath. Dropping the pink was almost a formality, but he didn't make the mistake of rushing it, waiting until the ball had actually tipped the edge of the pocket before stepping away from the table to receive the loser's gallant handshake and acknowledge the tumultuous applause.

'So we have a new World Champ!' exclaimed Sara's companion with some satisfaction. 'I said way back at the start of the season that he'd go far, but I never really anticipated this far this soon. First season as a pro and he clinches the big one!' He turned his head to glance at her, brows lifting. 'Not impressed? I thought you were as involved as anybody this last couple of frames.'

Sara smiled, her eyes on the group down below as the presentations were made. 'As a matter of fact, I was wondering how many of the women who watch snooker are as interested in the game itself as in the men who play it? Those outfits they wear do a lot for the male physique—particularly when they're leaning across the table for an awkward shot.'

Jeff Brady grinned. 'Maybe it's an angle worth pursuing.'

She pulled a face at him. 'I should have known better than to leave you with an opening like that.'

'Never miss an opportunity,' he agreed. 'Still, it isn't such a bad idea at that. You could even run a contest in that rag you write for—which player has the most appealing behind!'

'I've written for that rag *you* write for on more than one occasion,' she reminded him, ignoring the satire. 'Are you going down to have a word with the winner?'

'I'll see him at the party. His agent will set up a general press interview.'

'Supposing he'd lost?'

'They'd probably have given him a party anyway just for making it to the finals. He's won four major tournaments since September, that makes him valuable property. The commercial guys will be after him, you can bet. At thirty he's young enough to appeal to the kids, yet old enough to carry some weight with the rest too.'

'He played as an amateur before this season, of course?' Sara asked.

'Oh sure. Most of these guys have been playing since they were kids themselves.' He gave her a sharp glance. 'If you're thinking what I think you're thinking, then think again. You might have persuaded a few people to give you exclusives, but this one is another proposition. Believe me, it's been tried.'

Sara returned the look blandly. 'You mean he doesn't like talking about himself?'

'You said it! Outside of the game, his life is a closed book.'

'There's no such thing.'

'All right then, it's one he won't open himself. He'll talk about the game all you want, and he's worth listening to, but try delving any deeper and he clams up.'

Sara said softly, 'Perhaps there's something in his past that won't bear too much investigation.'

'Maybe, maybe not. I'd say it's more that he believes in personal privacy. The public's only entitled to the bit he puts on show, not the whole caboodle. Can't say I blame him too much for that.'

'Coming from a newspaper man, that's some admission,' she teased.

'A sportswriter,' he corrected. 'We're a different breed.'

'So you keep telling me.' She applauded along with the rest as the man in question lifted the cup above his head in a gesture of triumph, conscious of the little frisson of awareness as their eyes seemed to lock for a moment. Lit by a sudden gleam of mockery, the others lingered with brief deliberation before passing on, leaving her with an odd sense of having been weighed up and found wanting all in the space of a few seconds. Antagonism fought with intrigue, the latter winning by a short head because for her the job had to take priority over personal feelings. Resolve hardened. All right, Mr High and Mighty Lyness, she thought. Let's see what you're really made of!

The party was being held at a city-centre hotel. Dropped outside the main doors by the mini-bus in use by the press, Sara accompanied Jeff and the rest of the gang up in a lift to the reception area, there to be directed to a private room where celebrations were already in full swing.

Seizing a couple of glasses of champagne from a passing tray, Jeff passed one across to her and lifted the other in a laughing toast.

'Aren't you glad now that you came?' he shouted above the general hubbub of voices.

'Yes,' she shouted back. 'It's been a whole new experience!'

'Talking of which,' he murmured, putting his lips

closer to her ear, 'we still have the rest of the night ahead.'

'In separate rooms,' she reminded him, turning her head so he could see her lips forming the words. 'We settled that last night.'

'I'm ever hopeful,' he mouthed back, not particularly crestfallen. 'The night's still young.'

And the gesture made, Sara reflected. And that was all it had been. Jeff hadn't asked her along on this trip simply in the hope of getting her into bed—although he almost certainly wouldn't have thrown her out of it either had she shown willing. It was time she sampled something a little different, he had declared halfway through the week. How could she possibly tell whether snooker was her cup of tea or not until she had actually sat through a few frames of a championship match? Well, she had sat through them, and had not found the experience unenjoyable, she was bound to admit. The sheer, nail-biting tension of that final battle for supremacy could have left no one untouched. The two men had been so evenly matched. To win by one frame had to be better in many ways than winning by a dozen, because the challenge had been so much greater.

'Come and meet the Champ while there's still a chance,' Jeff said now, taking her by the arm. 'There are more people pouring in every minute.'

Sare went with him without protest, the glass held high to prevent spillage as they jostled their way through the milling crowd of well-wishers. The man in question was in the midst; yet not, she thought, really part of them. There was an air about him of aloofness, as if he were standing back mentally surveying the lesser mortals. Probably an unfair assessment, she acknowledged, when based on such scant knowledge.

Jeff was greeted by name, his congratulations

accepted in the same spirit in which they were offered. Drawing Sara forward, the sportswriter introduced the two of them, making no attempt to qualify the relationship. Meeting the amber-flecked green eyes, Sara thought she read cynicism in his appraisal. Apparent though it was what he was probably thinking, it didn't worry her particularly. Even if she and Jeff had been lovers taking advantage of a weekend together, it would have been nothing to do with this man.

Making allowances for her three-inch heels, he was taller than her own five feet six by a good seven inches. Tall enough, as Jeff had pointed out, to make getting down to the table difficult if his hips hadn't been so supple. Macho man, she thought amusedly, allowing her eyes to dwell for a moment on the firm jawline already showing a faint shading of blue. Given the opportunity to shave again for the party, he probably wouldn't have bothered. She doubted if he allowed any kind of inconsequentiality to bother him. His voice was good and deep and easy on the ear, the northern accent less marked than she had anticipated.

'I had a lucky break,' he said in answer to her murmured congratulations. 'It could have gone either way.'

'Spoken with true sportsmanship!' she responded lightly. 'Novice I might be at the game, but I can recognise a brilliant shot when I see it. That final blue ball was no fluke.'

Dave conceded the point with an ironic inclination of his head. 'Not just a pretty face!'

'Not even a pretty face,' she corrected. 'If you want to compliment a woman, call her attractive. Pretty is strictly for babies.'

'I'll remember that.' He reached out and took the half-empty glass from her fingers, replacing it with a full one from the tray offered by a waiter. 'It's best when it's fresh,' he said, 'more zing. Are you going to be staying around?'

'We'll be here to the bitter end,' Jeff promised for her before she could answer. 'Right now I think we'd better float, and give some of these others piling in a chance.'

'You made an impression,' he stated when they were out of earshot. 'He's got used to women falling over themselves to please. A real guy for the gals, is our new champ. Not that they last long, by all accounts.'

The initial noise had abated enough to make speech audible at close range. Sara smiled, taking a sip from the glass in her hand. 'I can imagine. Thanks for not telling him what I do for a living, by the way. It gives me some advantage.'

'You're still considering that angle?'

'Perhaps. He interests me as a subject.'

'Spoken with true professional objectivity,' he jeered. 'You'll be asking for trouble if you try taking that chappie to the cleaners—not that you'll be the only one trying. He's big news right now.'

'For at least forty-eight hours,' Sara agreed drily. 'I'm looking to longer-term interest.'

'How do you reckon on achieving anything before tomorrow morning? We're catching the ten fifty-five back to town.'

She met his gaze with bland assurance. 'Perhaps I might stay over for a day or two. After all, it's my first time in these parts. It would be a shame not to see a bit more of Yorkshire while I'm here.'

Jeff sighed and gave up. 'Be it on your head! Personally, I can't wait to get back to civilisation.'

'No stamina,' she retorted, unmoved. 'A good story is worth a little inconvenience.'

'Always provided you get it in the end.'

'I haven't failed up to now.'

'Nice to have your kind of confidence.'

On the surface at any rate, Sara acknowledged mentally, hiding a wry smile. Reticence cut no ice; she had learned that early on in life. What one wanted one went out and got, regardless of who might be hurt in the process. If way down deep she still held reservations on that score, then that was where they were staying. So far as other people were concerned, she was what she appeared to be—a career girl plain and simple. At twenty-three years of age she had already made something of a mark on the world, if only in the eyes of those who read a certain leading magazine. Dave Lyness wouldn't be one of them, she was reasonably sure, which meant her name wasn't likely to create any ripples in his memory circuits. All that remained now was to follow up her advantage.

Jeff helped by drifting off to talk with some other press members, leaving her sitting in a corner close by one of the windows overlooking the city streets. Dave came to join her, bringing a fresh glass of champagne along with him.

'I've had enough,' Sara told him, smiling into his face, 'but thanks, anyway.'

'No sweat,' he said, dropping into the chair at her side. 'It was only an excuse to come over.'

'You find you need one?' she asked lightly. 'You're the celebrity here. Nobody in their right mind is going to turn down a chance to bask in your reflected glory. How does it feel to be on top of the world after eight short months?'

'Eight months as a professional,' he corrected easily. 'Fourteen years in practice.'

'So you started playing when you were only sixteen?'

His eyes crinkled suddenly at the corners. 'You've been doing some homework.'

'Jeff said you were thirty now. Maths was never my best subject, but I can subtract reasonably well.'

'Puts us about on a par.' He studied her a moment, head tilted. 'I saw you in the Crucible back there at the end.'

'And passed me over,' she quipped.

'Not exactly passed, more a case of reserving for a later time. You were with Jeff Brady so I had a good idea you'd be coming along here. What's with you two? I wouldn't want to tread on any toes.'

Sara looked him straight in the eye. 'We're just good friends.'

'That can cover a lot of ground these days.'

'Not in our case. He thought I might like to see what the game was about at first hand, nothing more.'

'And?'

She smiled. 'I was fascinated. Until you really watch it, you don't realise how much skill goes into it. How much practice do you have to put in to keep on form?'

'I was doing ten hours a day coming up to this fortnight,' he admitted. 'Between playing for real, that is.' He settled deeper into the chair, slinging one ankle across the other knee to reveal an inch or two of bare, bronzed leg. 'Solarium,' he added, following her eyes and accurately guessing her passing thought. 'I've got my own. When you spend as much time inside as I do there's not much chance to even see the sun, much less lie in it. For fifteen minutes most mornings, when I'm home, I can imagine I'm stretched out on some exotic beach. Given the help of an electric fan, I can even create palm trees swaying in the breeze!'

Sara was laughing. 'You're obviously suffering from travel-lust!'

'I get plenty of travel, but one table looks much the same as another when they're all green. I'll be playing in Las Vegas next month. One of the perks of winning tonight. Did you ever visit the Grand Canyon?'

She shook her head. 'It's never been a particular ambition.'

'It should be. It's been one of mine since I was a kid.'

There was a small pause. Sara was the first to break it, voice casual. 'Are any of your family here tonight?'

'My brother.' He waved a hand. 'Over there, somewhere.'

'You don't have anyone else?'

'They'll have been watching it on television.' He said it without particular inflection but something seemed to close up in his face. 'How about you? Do you live in London?'

'I have a flat in St John's Wood,' she acknowledged.

'Secretary to some business tycoon, I suppose.'

It was more of an ironical remark than a question; Sara let it stand, lifting her shoulders in a smiling shrug. 'Somebody has to perform the mundane tasks.'

'Not tomorrow though,' he observed. 'Which train are you planning on catching back?'

Her heartbeat suddenly increased its pace, almost as if she had been running. 'As a matter of fact,' she said, 'I was thinking of taking a couple of days extra to see something of the area while I'm up here. I've been told there's some lovely countryside within easy reach. I'll be hiring a car. Perhaps you can give me some ideas on where to go?'

'I can do better than that,' came the hoped-for, though not entirely anticipated, reply. 'I'll show you myself, if you like.'

The hesitation was nicely timed. 'Won't you be tied up with press and publicity people?'

'I can't be if I'm not around. I merit a couple of days off anyway. There's nothing pressing before Pontin's next week.'

'A holiday camp?'

'One of them. It's the annual snooker festival. All the pros will be there—plus about a thousand amateurs for the Open.' He shook his head. 'We're getting away from the point. How about it?'

'All right, fine. I couldn't have a better guide than a local.'

Somebody called Dave's name, waving an arm at him over the intervening heads. He pulled a face, bringing himself upright in the chair. 'Looks like I'd better start circulating again. Are you staying right here in the hotel?'

'Yes.' She gave him a straight glance. 'Separate rooms.'

'I'm no moralist,' he denied. 'Anyway, I believed you the first time. I'll pick you up at ten-thirty, give us time to drive round a bit before we eat. Any preferences? I'm a pub man myself.'

'Good enough for me too,' she said. 'Good night, Dave.'

'You mean morning, don't you?' He rested a hand lightly on her shoulder in passing her chair, fingers momentarily curving the bone in a touch that sent a sudden tremor down her spine. 'See you.'

It was past one-thirty. Considering that the final hadn't finished until almost midnight, she supposed the time hadn't really gone that fast; it only seemed so. Her mind still retained an image of Dave Lyness's face, so uncompromisingly masculine; the green eyes too perceptive for comfort. He had a sensualist's mouth, the lower lip long and curved faintly downwards at the corners in repose. A mouth to tantalise, to taunt, to inspire a certain yearning in any female with normal responses—and Sara's responses were very normal indeed. She would have to remind herself, and keep on reminding herself, exactly why she was seeing the man again. No mere physical attraction could be allowed to come between her and her aims.

Jeff appeared at her elbow as she made for the outer

door of the room. 'Going already?' he asked. 'The night just got started!'

'Not for me,' she denied. 'I've had it.'

'You mean you lost the incentive to stay.' The grin registered her faint change of expression. 'I saw you in confab with Dave over there. Guess everybody did. What about that train tomorrow?'

This time Sara kept her facial muscles strictly under control. 'I'm staying. See you back in town.'

'Good luck,' he called after her. 'You'll need it.'

It wasn't luck she needed so much as a steady nerve, she reflected, resuming her course for the door. The main problem was going to be at which point she told Dave who and what she was. If she could gain his trust she might also gain his co-operation. A profile needed insight to make any impact at all.

The morning was fine and sunny, though with a cool easterly breeze. Sara put on a warm, cowl-necked sweater in cream along with a brown-and-cream checked skirt, sliding her feet into low-heeled pumps. Dressed for the country, she thought amusedly, viewing her reflection through the mirror before leaving the room. It was fortunate that she never travelled without a small selection of clothes for all occasions when she wasn't quite sure what was going to be called for, having been caught out a time or two in the past. A two-day weekend watching snooker for the most part had seemed a pretty safe bet, but the habit had persisted. Whatever the coming couple of days might throw up, she was prepared.

Jeff was already at breakfast when she got down to the restaurant. She went to join him, shaking her head in answer to the waitress's inquiry.

'Just coffee and toast for me, thanks.'

Jeff squinted at her painfully through bleary eyes as he lifted his own refilled cup to his lips. 'Do you have to look so darned bright and breezy at this ungodly hour?' he groaned.

Sara regarded him with some lack of sympathy. 'What time did you get to bed?'

'Lord only knows. It seemed like only minutes before the wake-up call came through. So far as I can remember, a couple of us tried drinking the flags—you know, mixing all the different national colours. We got stuck on Germany. Couldn't find anything black apart from Guinness, and they'd run out.'

Sara shuddered. 'Perhaps it's as well. Do you think you'll make it to the train?'

'It's only just down the road to the station. I might even walk it. It'd clear my head.' He took another gulp of coffee and seemed to gain some inner strength, viewing her with an awakening of interest. 'Still planning on pinning Lyness to the board?'

'Not in the sense you're suggesting. I only publish what I'm given permission to publish. Too many pitfalls otherwise.'

'You mean you'll tell him what you're after?'

She smiled a little. 'Eventually I'll have to. That rag I write these things for insists on full authentication from the subject before they publish any profile.'

'Honourable of them.'

'More a case of safety first. People aren't always keen on being seen the way others see them, and the libel laws can cover a lot of ground.'

'True.' He glanced at his watch, drained the last of his coffee and pushed back his chair. 'I'd better think about checking out if I'm going to make that train. Lucky I travel light. You'd have a job lugging that case of yours a couple of feet, much less a mile!'

'Except that I wouldn't be needing to clear my head by walking in the first place,' she retorted sweetly. 'Pleasant journey, Jeff.'

The restaurant was only a quarter full. Monday

morning was a quiet time for most hotels, she
supposed; the weekenders already gone, the business
travellers not yet arrived. In half an hour Dave Lyness
would be waiting for her out there in the lobby. No
doubt he'd be recognised: one of the city's own sons
come to fame and fortune. Jeff had been right about
his commercial prospects. He had it made.

She stopped at the desk on her way out to extend
her stay by a couple of nights. Working freelance gave
her the kind of flexibility she preferred, although it
had been a bit of a gamble to start with. Not that she
was so desperate for money. Invested, the legacy left
her by her grandmother covered adequate living
expenses. All the same, it was good to know the
capability was there. Once she had built up sufficient
financial security she might get down to producing
that book she kept turning over in her mind. Another
gamble, considering the number of writers already in
the saga market, but something she had to try
regardless.

Dave was standing over by the lifts when she went
down again on the half-hour. He was wearing casual
slacks in dark brown together with a creamy wool
sweater.

'Snap!' Sara exclaimed as she came into earshot.
'We obviously favour the same colours.'

'It's a good start,' he agreed. 'Are you going to be
warm enough without a coat? There's a nip in the air
still.'

'I'll be all right in the car,' she said, then tilted her
head. 'Unless you were planning on some other form
of transport.'

His smile came easily. 'My bus days were over a
long time ago. Ready to go?'

He was parked on a meter just round the corner
from the lower entrance. Sara viewed the racy, dark
red Rover with some appreciation. Dave opened the

passenger door first and waited until she was seated
before making for his own side of the car. She caught a
faint whiff of aftershave as he slid into his seat, subtle
and emotive. Not Brut, thank God, more Estée
Lauder. So much for preconceptions! Northern men
weren't so very different when it came right down to
it. The vowels might be flat, but so far she hadn't seen
even one Andy Capp.

Dave was silent as he negotiated the busy Monday
morning traffic. Only when they were heading out
through the suburbs did he finally glance her way.

'Comfortable?' he asked.

'Absolutely,' she said. 'You can't have had this
long.'

'A couple of months. My last car was a three-year-
old Capri.'

'A measure of your success then. The sky's the limit
now.'

'So they tell me.' His tone was dry. 'I'll have to
make the most of it while it lasts.'

Sara gave him a sideways look. 'You don't see
yourself retaining the title next year?'

He shrugged. 'In this game there's no certainty of
any kind. Some of the younger players coming up are
likely to give us all a run for our money. With
unemployment the way it is, a lot of them have more
time to get in practice.'

She said softly, 'More than you had when you were
their age?'

'Quite a bit. At sixteen I was an apprentice
bricklayer.'

'So you were interested in the building trade?'

'Only because I didn't fancy the steelworks.' His
lips twisted. 'Even way back then you needed more
than a couple of indifferent O-levels to get anywhere.'

'If you could do it again would you stay on in
school, do you think?'

'With hindsight, sure. I'd do a whole lot of things differently.'

Sara would have liked to delve deeper, but enough had to be enough for the present. Her mental file was already off to a good start. She was glad she had resisted the temptation when Dave went silent again, as if he were conscious of having been drawn further than he had intended. He was wary, but of what? Ashamed of his background, perhaps? Yet he didn't seem the type. There had been no reticence in what he had said, just that bare hint of regret.

The road had widened out and taken on a residential aspect, with traditionally designed houses facing an open park; trees decorated both pavements. Through a set of lights, and the houses gave way to thick woods and then eventually to houses again, this time with almost a village atmosphere about the setting. The road began to climb, passing between fields edged by dry-stone walls. Green hills lofted in all directions.

'Derbyshire,' Dave stated a few minutes later as they topped the last rise on a magnificent view of a wide, lush valley. 'You're seeing it at its best, on a weekday during term time. Come summer weekends it's nose to tail with traffic. Sheffield folk love their countryside—sometimes to extremes.'

'It's beautiful,' Sara declared, and drew an ironic glance.

'You don't have to make appropriate noises. Just relax and enjoy it.'

She laughed suddenly. 'You know, you're not a bit what I expected!'

'Cloth cap and braces?'

'Well, perhaps not quite that far. I thought you might be one of those strong, silent types.'

'Inarticulate is the word you're looking for. I probably was at one time, but they say travel broadens the mind. I did a lot of it with the amateur league before I turned pro.'

'You stayed in the building trade all those years between?' Sara ventured.

A faint line appeared between his brows. 'Not all of them, no. Anyway, that's enough about me. How about you?'

'There isn't much to tell.' Her head was back against the rest, her attention apparently captured by the unfolding scene ahead. 'I was born in Surrey. My parents divorced when I was twelve, and I lived with my mother till I finished school, then moved to London.'

'Big place for a girl on her own.'

'I coped.'

'I'm sure you did.' There was no trace of mockery in his voice. 'No ties at all?'

'If you mean men,' she said, 'then the answer is no. I'm footloose and fancy free, as the saying goes!'

'Something else we have in common.'

She said slyly, 'Not a common occurrence for you, though, from what I hear. Jeff told me you were "quite a guy for the gals", to put it in his own Yankee-style jargon.'

'Exaggeration. My time's too limited.' He slanted a glance. 'Anyway, there's women and women. You're hardly run-of-the-mill.'

A faint warning bell sounded at the back of Sara's mind as nerve and sinew tautened pleasurably. She was becoming more and more attracted to this man, and not just physically either. She liked being with him, liked talking with him. There was a quality in him that she hadn't found in any other man.

Two days, she reminded herself. You're only going to be here two days.

CHAPTER THREE

THAT first day went by far too quickly. They lunched at a small, stone-built public house in an unspoilt village, then drove out as far as Youlgreave for tea. In the course of the afternoon, Sara learned little more about Dave's background but quite a lot about the man himself. He was, she found, totally unpretentious with regard to his leisure-time pursuits. Book-reading was confined to the occasional Robert Ludlum or Desmond Bagley, his taste in music middle-of-the-road. Outside of snooker itself, rugby and golf were his main sporting interests, the one to watch and follow, the other actually to play when opportunity arose, although lack of practice scarcely improved his handicap. Politically they proved much of the same mind: out for the best compromise, as Dave himself put it—a word which Sara imagined he didn't apply to his own affairs too often.

'What about tonight?' he asked when they were almost back to town. 'Dinner for starters?'

With what to follow? she wondered fleetingly, then shelved the thought as unworthy of the moment. Ulterior motives aside, she wanted to say yes.

He allowed her a couple of hours' respite. Sara took advantage of them to use the bath instead of the shower, stretching out luxuriously in scented foam bubbles and allowing her thoughts to drift back over the day. She had enjoyed every minute, and so, she was sure, had Dave. Mentally they were well matched; physically they were without doubt equally drawn. The question was, where could it lead? They moved in different worlds along paths which were unlikely to cross again. She wasn't even sure she would want them to when it came right down to it. Her career was the most most important thing in her life at present. Whether it would always be so remained open to speculation. Keeping Dave at arm's length might not be easy but it was going to be expedient. She couldn't afford to become involved, not when eventual confession was in the offing.

They went to a small Italian restaurant just out of the city centre. From outside the place looked nothing much, but both interior décor and menu made up for it. Certainly the prices were high enough, Sara reflected, settling in the end for the Tournedos Rossini.

'Nice,' she said, smiling at the man seated across from her at the intimately lit table for two. 'Definitely up-market.'

'I was just thinking the same thing,' he returned. 'You look like a brunette Princess Di in that outfit!'

Sara put up a hand to touch the little frill at the throat of her white silk blouse. 'Flattery,' she said lightly, 'is music to my ears.'

'I doubt it,' his voice had a dry note, 'but it was worth a try.'

She lifted a quizzical eyebrow. 'Softening me up for something?'

The grin was fleeting. 'Not noticeably.'

He didn't know the half of it, she thought, aware of his impact in the dark grey suit and shadow-striped shirt. Her pulses told a story best kept to herself, considering the circumstances.

The atmosphere didn't help, of course. Nor did the heady Chianti they drank with the meal. As the evening progressed, Sara could feel herself mellowing; feel priorities altering as matter took over from mind. Dave attracted her deeply, too deeply to ignore, but that nothing could come of it hardly seemed important at the moment. It was enough to be with him, to watch his face as they talked, seeing the way his eyes crinkled at the corners when he laughed, the fall of lamplight on strong male cheek bones, the slow and sensual curl of that lower lip as he watched her watching him. She couldn't find it in herself to care overmuch about what she might be giving away. No man had ever affected her quite like this before. It was like falling headfirst down a helter-skelter.

Somehow she found herself telling him about her childhood, about the trauma of the divorce.

'I hated my father for putting another woman before us,' she admitted, 'yet I suppose my mother was as much to blame for not being able to hold him. When she married again I just had to get away. I go to see her from time to time, of course, but usually when Roger is away on a business trip.'

'What about your father?' asked Dave. 'Do you see anything of him?'

Sara shrugged. 'He's never shown much inclination towards getting together. With a new young family of his own, I suppose he feels it easier to let things lie. I've got over it now.'

'I don't think so,' Dave said softly. He reached across and took her hand in a gesture totally devoid of self-consciousness, his thumb gently brushing her knuckles as he held it. 'Hurt like that gets pushed under cover but it doesn't go away.'

She could feel the tensile strength of his long, lean fingers across her palm, the touch smooth and warm. Plain gold links clasped the white cuff about a wrist lightly covered in hair that glinted several shades paler than the thick sweep on his head, contrasting with the tan of his skin. Her own skin tingled everywhere, almost as if he were stroking her whole body.

'Did you?' she heard herself asking. 'Ever get hurt, I mean?'

'We've all been through it one way or another,' came the evasive reply. 'Did you want coffee here, or shall we go back to my place?'

She was being a fool, and she knew it, but it made little difference. She wasn't drunk, she told herself, only slightly intoxicated, and Dave was hardly the type to force his attentions on an unwilling partner. What harm was there in a cup of coffee—maybe even a little light lovemaking, if it came to that? Her mouth ached for the feel of his lips.

Their destination lay in one of the city's better-class suburbs. He left her sitting in the flat's living-room while he went to make the coffee, returning to find her looking through a selection of tapes in a cabinet beside the stereo.

'Put one on if you can find something you like,' he invited, setting down the tray he was carrying. 'I'll let you do the pouring.'

'A woman's work?' she queried with faint irony. 'I'd have made it too if you'd asked.'

'Don't worry,' he returned equably, 'I would another time.'

Except that there was hardly going to be another time, reflected Sara, already sobered by the ride here. Some time within the next twenty-four hours she was going to have to tell Dave the truth. If there was any chance at all of persuading him to grant her the background detail she still needed, it would depend on how she handled things tonight. Coming home with him was a mistake. It put their relationship on a different footing. Perhaps her best bet might even be to make the confession here and now before any further misunderstandings could arise.

'It's a nice place you have,' she said, slotting a selection from *Porgy and Bess* into the recorder and switching on. 'Does your family live close?'

'About five miles as the crow flies,' he responded,

'across the other side of the city. I only moved here a few months ago after the money started coming in.'

She sat down on the sofa and began pouring the coffee before tagging on casually, 'You lived at home up till then.'

'No,' he acknowledged, taking the cup from her. 'I moved out when I was in my early twenties.'

Sara smiled. 'Too restrictive on your love-life?'

'Could be.' He was smiling himself, giving little away. 'A bachelor flat certainly helped.'

'I'll bet.' She was trying to imagine him at twenty-two, twenty-three, failing because the image he created now was too intrusive. His closeness on the sofa beside her was having its effect. Her hand was unsteady as she lifted her own cup to her lips. 'Good coffee,' she commented, trying to ignore what was happening to her insides.

'Thanks.' He sounded amused. 'I don't normally bother with the real stuff. Too much trouble.'

'To switch on a percolator?'

'*And* wait ten minutes for it to perk. By that time I've lost interest.'

'You mean with you it's now or never.' The statement was idle, the challenge unintentional. She sensed his reaction and stiffened a little, looking for a way to retract. Only it was too late because he was reaching for her cup, taking it from her unresisting fingers to set it down alongside his own on the table before them.

'It's as good a policy as any,' he murmured, drawing her towards him.

His mouth was a torment, making up in passion what it might lack in tenderness. Sara found herself responding in kind, her fingers creeping up to bury themselves in the thickness of his hair, her body moving forward in a rising, overwhelming urge for contact. He pulled her across him, turning her so that she lay with her head pillowed against his upper arm, leaving her mouth to kiss his way down the line of her throat and reach the vulnerable hollow where the pulse beat so wildly.

'I've thought about this since the first minute I clapped eyes on you,' he said softly, lifting his head a little to look into her bemused and bewitched face. 'Of all the folk in that auditorium last night, you were the only one who looked totally unimpressed.'

'I *was* impressed,' she whispered, 'desperately! I'm even more so now.'

His laugh came low. 'We only just got started.'

She closed her eyes as he traced a line with one finger along her jaw to her ear, drawing in her breath at the erotic exploration of sensitive tissue. Without thinking about it, she slid a hand between the buttons of his shirt, finding wiry hair and bare, warm skin. He carried no spare weight, just hard, flat muscle, the latter contracting where her fingers touched. She wanted to be closer, to feel flesh against flesh.

When he unfastened her blouse and bared her breasts she couldn't wait to do the same for him, burying her face in his chest with a blind urgency. His skin tasted salty, the hair tickling her tongue. She felt his hand lift her chin, the pressure once more of his lips, the tingling brush of his tongue as he sought and gained response. Her breasts were touching the wall of his chest, but not crushed by it, the nipples hardened to taut peaks of desire. There had never been a sensation to match this, she thought hazily, answering the demanding kisses with a wildness growing by the minute. Never!

It took the slow sliding movement of his hand along her thigh to restore her to sanity. Even then it was all she could do to break free of the need coursing through her own veins. Dave made no attempt to stop her as she slid abruptly from his arms and stood up;

his breathing was roughened but there was no loss of control. Sara didn't dare glance his way as she fumbled the buttons of her blouse closed again.

'I'm sorry,' she said, low-toned, 'that was my fault. I let the whole thing go too far.'

'It takes two,' he said after a moment. 'Why did you change your mind?'

Her shoulders lifted in a wry little shrug. 'Would you believe I'm not in the habit of doing this kind of thing?'

'Going to bed with a man you hardly know? Yes, I'd believe it. That still doesn't answer the question.'

She made herself turn back to look at him, meeting the green eyes with a sense of shame that had little to do with the immediate situation. He was sitting with one arm resting along the sofa back, his shirt still open to the waist. His tie lay where she herself had dropped it on the floor.

'It wasn't because I didn't want to,' she said thickly, and saw his lips turn down at one corner.

'I realise that.'

'So help me out,' she appealed, 'just let it go.'

'On one condition,' he said. 'You were going to stay over a couple of days. Don't run away because we got off the mark too soon.'

Sara gazed at him indecisively, not at all sure what it was she wanted. 'Is one day going to make any difference?'

'It is to me.' His smile was slow but devoid of mockery. 'We'll spend it any way you want.'

The temptation was double-edged, and it took an effort to bring her priorities back in line. 'You'd normally be keeping your hand in for this tournament next week, wouldn't you? It must be important for you to cement your image by continuing to win.'

'True,' he conceded. 'I'd like the professional title, at any rate. Nobody wants a pro to win the Open.' He tagged on comfortably, 'There'll be plenty of time after you've left.'

'I'd like to watch you for an hour or two,' she said quickly. 'That is, if you wouldn't mind an audience.'

'Hardly.' He was viewing her with a certain scepticism. 'Are you serious?'

'Never more.' She kept her tone light. 'Like a whole lot of others, I'm hooked on the game. You could show me some of those trick shots I've heard about for starters.'

'I didn't have you pegged as a real enthusiast,' Dave admitted. 'But you're more than welcome if . . .' He broke off as the telephone rang, mouth slanting. 'It had to be too good to last—although I suppose the timing could have been worse.'

Sara began clearing the used crockery back on to the tray as he went to answer it. Even from where she was across the room she heard the splutter of sound from the other end of the line before Dave had finished saying the number. He listened patiently for a number of seconds before making any attempts to break in on the tirade.

'Take it easy, Roy. I don't need that kind of publicity.' He paused again, added on a shorter note, 'Okay, so I don't want it. The people who matter are impressed by results, not commercial coverage. We already agreed no promotion contracts. No, I haven't changed my mind. Davis already cornered the market in that line.'

Carrying the tray through to the kitchen, Sara filled the bowl with hot water and slid in the cups and saucers. She had them stacked on the drying-rack by the time Dave followed her in.

'You didn't have to bother with those,' he said, 'they'd have kept. I've a woman comes in Tuesdays and Fridays to clean the place.'

'It didn't take two minutes.' She gave him an assessing glance. 'Trouble?'

He shrugged. 'That was my agent. Seems he's been trying to get in touch most of the day. He wants me to take on a commercial promotion.'

'And you're against that kind of thing?'

'Not exactly against it, just not interested. I want to play snooker, not stand around grinning into TV cameras!'

'There's a lot of money in it.'

'And a lot of aggro too. If I start running short I'll get somebody to ghost my life story, the way everybody else does.'

Sara waited a brief moment before commenting on that one, damping down her initial reaction. 'That doesn't sound a bad idea.'

'It's a lousy idea.' He came over and took the tea-towel from her, pinning it back on its hook. 'Leave them.'

She obeyed without argument, standing with her back against the sink unit to view the strong male features with concealed exasperation. 'Why is it a lousy idea? As you just said, other winners have done it.'

'Too many. That's why I'd rather stay out of it. Anyway ...' He stopped and shrugged, expression closed. 'It was just a passing joke.'

Whatever her own ideas on the subject, Sara conceded reluctantly, now was not the time to discuss them. 'I think I ought to get back to the hotel,' she said instead.

Dave stood his ground as she moved to pass him, taking her arm and turning to face him. 'One for the road,' he said softly, and it wasn't a question.

Held close up against that lean, hard body, Sara fought her inclinations and kept the kiss cool. All the same, he was smiling when he let her go.

'I'm glad you decided to stay on,' he stated.

'Tomorrow's a whole new day.'

'Philosophy at this hour?' she taunted, but there was no malice in it. His very touch made her limbs feel weak. One hand came up of its own will to his mouth, her forefinger tracing the line of his lower lip. 'I believe you could be cruel if you wanted to be. A merciless opponent!'

'You're hardly likely to come up against that side of me,' he responded, not denying it. 'Let's go, while I still have the mind.'

He came in with her when they reached the hotel, suggesting a nightcap in the bar. This time they weren't so lucky. Over the space of the next half-hour at least a dozen people came over to offer congratulations, several asking for autographs. Dave took it all in good part, exchanging a few words, the odd joke, his whole manner easy.

'I imagine all that could become very wearing after a time,' Sara commented when the last one had gone.

He shrugged. 'Maybe, but it doesn't cost much to be pleasant to people. Fans keep the game going. Would you like another drink?'

She shook her head. 'Not for me, thanks. I feel quite tired. Must be all that fresh air today!'

'You hardly got out of the car,' he scoffed, rising with her. 'A good hike across Kinder Scout is what you need.'

'If that's as rugged as it sounds, I'll take a raincheck,' she came back, then laughed. 'Now I'm starting to sound like Jeff!'

'You should come with me to Vegas,' Dave said idly. 'You could put it to good use then.'

Joke or not, the notion made her heart jerk. She made no reply because the remark hadn't called for one. Out in the lobby again he said he would come for her at nine, gave her a swift, unsatisfying kiss and departed without a backward glance.

So much for not getting involved, Sara thought wryly, going up in the lift. Everything Dave said, everything he did, took her in deeper. She had to fight that attraction if she was to get anywhere at all. Journalists couldn't afford too much of a conscience when it came to ferreting out a story.

Except that right now the game hardly seemed that important. There were other stories she could write, other celebrities she could chase. As a freelance she was at liberty to choose her own assignments: Dave didn't have to be one of them. Why shouldn't he retain the privacy that appeared to be so important to him? It was an angle to consider, even if only for her own peace of mind.

The decision was made before she slept. Tomorrow she was going to forget her job and concentrate on enjoying the short time left before her return home. Beyond that she didn't attempt to contemplate. There wasn't, she supposed, a great deal of point.

The billiard hall where Dave Lyness, among others, had first become hooked on the game had long since been demolished as part of the city's East End improvement campaign. His present home-from-home took up the whole top floor of what had once been a large warehouse overlooking the canal. Painted a drab brown, the vast room was anything but prepossessing. A dozen tables, the majority of them already occupied, attracted the main sources of light from the overhead fluorescents.

Dave was greeted from all sides with friendly banter, although no one, Sara noted, lost much time in getting back to their game. Introduced to the portly, balding little man who owned the place, she weathered a brief but speculative inspection before he turned his attention back to Dave again.

'Expected you yesterday,' he said, 'so did the

press. Round here like flies in a milk bottle, they were!'

Dave grinned. 'I escaped. Usual table?'

'Where else?' He added, 'I'll fetch your lady friend a comfy chair. She'd find these a bit hard.'

'Does he usually refer to people in the third person when they're standing right there?' asked Sara in amusement as the little man moved off towards his office.

'Joe finds women hard to talk to at the best of times,' Dave responded equably. 'That posh accent of yours doesn't help.'

She gave him a swift glance. 'It doesn't seem to bother you.'

'That's because I'm more interested in the source than the sound.' He lifted a mocking eyebrow at the flicker of expression across her face. 'I can turn the odd phrase on occasion.'

'So I'm beginning to learn.' Her eyes were bright, clear blue. 'Not just a pretty face!'

He laughed, bunching his knuckle to push her gently under the chin. 'That's one I owe you.'

Threat or promise, it came out the same way, Sara acknowledged, registering the heady ebullience of the moment. She was suddenly thankful for last night's decision. Dave deserved better than to be used. The thought of going back to London tomorrow was not attractive. Yet she had no reason for staying longer. None, at least, that could be called reasonable. Nothing could come of this relationship. She had her life and he had his. She had to keep that in the forefront of her mind.

Seated on shabby but comfortable leather, she watched him set up the frame. At first he played what seemed a normal game, putting down several balls at speed and with what appeared to be scant attention for an initial break of sixteen before exhausting the easily

available pots. After that he appeared to get into
difficulties. Only gradually did Sara realise that he was
actually playing a dual game, anticipating the safety
shots an opponent might make in order to present
himself with a whole series of problems to solve. One
or two newcomers waiting for a table drifted over to
view proceedings with critical eyes, commenting
audibly from time to time and not always in flattering
style. Dave paid no attention. His concentration was
wholly on the table. When he miscued a shot he reset
it and tried again, sometimes taking as much as ten
minutes to achieve satisfaction. For the first time, Sara
began to appreciate that cue ball control was what the
game was all about, not just in potting the object-ball
aimed for but in placing the former in the most
advantageous position for the next shot.

Time passed quickly enough, and when Dave
straightened from a final zinging black the length of
the table, she was almost disappointed. The initial if
fleeting blankness in his gaze as their eyes met brought
a faint wry smile to her lips.

'You forgot I was here,' she accused.

'One of the hazards,' he admitted, not in the least
discomfited by the situation. 'A matter of priorities at
the time. Enjoying yourself?'

'As a matter of fact, yes,' she said, glad that the last
of the audience had gone to claim their own vacated
table. 'I'm even beginning to pick up some idea of how
you do what you're doing. Loosely speaking, it all
rests on at just which point and with how much
strength you strike the cue ball.'

'In a nutshell.' He paused, brows lifting inquiringly.
'How about having a go yourself?'

'Here?'

'I can't think of a better place.' He wasn't about to
let her off the hook, that was obvious from the glint in
his eyes. 'Choose yourself a cue from the rack. Mine's

going to be too heavy for you.' The pause held a taunt. 'Not scared, are you?'

'Dubious,' she said, getting reluctantly to her feet. 'I'll probably rip the baize, or something equally dreadful!'

'No, you won't. That only happens in films.' He went with her to the cue rack, weighing her choice in his hand. 'Seems about right.'

Back at the table he lined up the cue ball with a red placed a foot or so away from a corner pocket and stood back. 'Okay, let's see what you do with that.'

With everyone else in the place at present involved in playing their own games, Sara felt confident enough to at least make some attempt. Bending, she made a bridge with her left hand on the baize cloth, sighted along the cue until she thought she had the white in perfect line with the red, then eased back and struck. Instead of the good clean click Dave had produced, there was an unhealthy-sounding clunk and the cue ball jumped a visible inch in the air before rolling away at a tangent that took it well clear of the red to thud into the cushion.

'Damn!' she exclaimed wryly. 'What did I do wrong?'

'You had the butt raised too high so you dug down into the ball instead of striking it horizontally.' Dave lined up the balls again, then took the cue from her and laid it on the table with the butt towards her. 'Now pick it up as if you were going to hit somebody over the head with it, only without tensing your wrist and hand muscles.' He watched her do it, adding, 'That's the grip you should always use. Any tighter and your whole arm will tense up. Now the bridge.' He took her left hand and placed it almost flat on the table, spreading each finger and cocking her thumb. 'Nice and steady. Bend from the hips, not the waist, left leg forward and slightly bent, right leg straight to

give you stability. That's fine. Bring your chin down
close to the cue and sight with both eyes through the
middle of the cue ball to the red. How does that feel?'

He was still holding her hips in a firm grasp, body
following the line of hers so that he could size up the
shot as near as possible over her shoulder. Sara
managed a strangled assent, both relieved and
deprived when he moved away from her.
Concentrating fiercely, she drew back the cue in a
straight line and then forward again smoothly, hearing
the double click like music in her ears as the red rolled
into the pocket.

'Nice cueing,' applauded Dave. 'We'll make a player
of you yet!'

'You're hardly going to have time,' she came back,
smiling with sheer pleasure at her success—an
emotion which faded a little as her own words came
into sharper focus. 'I'll be on my way home at this
time tomorrow,' she tagged on lamely.

'London isn't the other end of the earth,' he
responded on a mild note. 'We can see each other again.'

He didn't ask if it was what she wanted. Noting it,
Sara wasn't at all sure what she would have answered.
Dave was like no other man she knew; he fascinated
her, captivated her. Physically and mentally they were
well tuned, only was that enough to overcome the
other differences in their make-up?

She was jumping too far ahead, she decided at that
point, shaking off the introspective mood. So what if
Dave did come down to London? What if they did
spend a little time together on occasion? It didn't have
to run to anything serious. She met the green eyes,
feeling the familiar tension in the pit of her stomach.
She had known handsomer men; why should this
one's looks affect her so strongly?

The sound of his name shouted from the other end
of the hall cut off any reply she might have made. The

young man making his way towards them from the direction of the main doors was younger than Dave by several years, but the resemblance was too marked to be missed.

'Thought you might be here,' the newcomer announced. 'Tried yesterday as well.' His eyes shifted briefly to Sara and away again. 'Suppose you had better things to do than come to see Mom and Dad.'

'My brother, Robert,' said Dave, apparently unmoved by the implied criticism. 'Sara Mellor.'

The younger man nodded awkwardly. 'Hallo.' Without pausing for any reply, he tagged on, 'Mom was expecting you all day. All the neighbours were waiting as well. She's real cut up about it.'

'That's a shame,' came the smooth reply. 'She'll get over it. Tell her I'll be there tomorrow.'

'Please, don't put it off for my sake,' Sara cut in. 'I can always do some shopping this afternoon.'

'Why don't you bring her with you?' suggested Robert with a sudden glint in his eye. 'It's got to be this afternoon. She's going to Brid' tomorrow.'

Dave reached out and took Sara's cue from her to put it back in the rack, expression unreadable. 'I've already made other plans.'

'I don't mind,' Sara said again, not sure if she was doing the right thing. 'I'd like to meet your family.'

Dave had his back to her. The pause before he turned away from the rack was only momentary but it showed. There was a certain resignation in the eyes meeting hers. 'Why not?' To his brother he added, 'We'll be there after lunch.'

From the look on his face, Robert was on the verge of some caustic comment, but he apparently thought better of it, saying instead, 'I'm going on afternoons straight from here, so you'll have to tell her yourself. Going to give me a game before you go, or are you too big for that now?'

'There isn't going to be time,' Dave pointed out. 'Not if we're going to eat. I booked a table for twelve-thirty.' He glanced back to Sara. 'Hope you like Chinese?'

'Love it,' she said truthfully, although not for anything would she have let him down in front of the younger man. 'It's almost twenty past now. Shouldn't we be making a move?'

'I'll phone the house first,' he said, 'and let them know we're coming.'

Sara watched him move away in the direction of the office, admiring his lean physique in the well-cut slacks and toning sweater. 'You must be very proud of him,' she said with some deliberation to Robert. 'Are you planning to follow in his footsteps?'

'Fat chance of that with a full-time job!'

'Dave managed it.'

'Yeah, well, he had all the luck, didn't he?'

'Oh, I think there has to be more to it than just luck. I imagine he had to spend the vast majority of his spare time building up his game.'

'He always found time for the birds,' came the sly reply. 'Different one every week, that's our Dave!'

'It's the only way for a bachelor to live,' Sara responded, refusing to allow the dig to get to her. 'No ties, no commitments. Marriage might have robbed him of his career.'

'He nearly got married once, only she chucked him for somebody else.'

'Really?' She kept her tone light. 'That can't have been pleasant for him.'

'He's a good catch now, though.' The pause was meaningful. 'For some, anyway.'

'For anyone,' she said without altering expression. 'Are you married, Robert?'

'No fear! I like a good time.'

'Who doesn't?' She left it there, relieved to see Dave coming back. 'That was quick!'

'No point in keeping it going when I'll be seeing them in a couple of hours.' He picked up the jacket of her dark red suit, holding it ready for her arms. 'As you said, it's time we weren't here.'

Easing her shoulders into the jacket, she felt his fingertips brush her nape, creating an area of tingling warmth. She could feel Robert's eyes on the pair of them; sense the derisory expression. Sibling jealousy was one thing she had never had to contend with, being an only child, yet she could to a certain extent understand it. Dave was leading the kind of life Robert would probably give his eye-teeth to emulate. Only it took more than just the wish.

CHAPTER FOUR

SARA waited until they were seated in the restaurant and halfway down an initial drink before saying tentatively, 'I hope I wasn't pushing you into anything you didn't want to do when I said I'd come with you this afternoon. It just seemed the easiest way out.'

'It probably was,' Dave agreed drily. 'You took the wind out of Rob's sails, at any rate.'

'It wasn't noticeable.'

'Take my word for it.'

She studied him a moment, registered the faint curl of his lip. 'Envy can be soul-destroying,' she murmured.

'Whose soul? Everything I've got I worked for.' The curl became a curve, infinitely more effective in its effect on her heartstrings. 'You're the only thing that fell into my lap recently.'

She pulled a face. 'You make it sound as if I deliberately set my cap at you!'

'Not quite, but I'm damned sure you didn't stay on just to satisfy my ego either. We've a lot going for us, Sara. Don't let anything spoil it.'

She said candidly, 'You're talking about this afternoon, aren't you? What are you afraid of, Dave? That I'm going to look down on your family because they're working-class?'

'If I felt like that,' he said on a suddenly harder note, 'we wouldn't be sitting here at all. *I'm* working-class. I'm no more ashamed of it than I'm unduly proud of it. It just happens to be.'

'So I had it wrong. Sorry.' She kept her tone reasonable. 'You can't deny you were reluctant to let me meet them. What else was I to think?'

The shrug was brief. 'Let's just leave it at that for now. Draw your own conclusions later. Did you settle on what you're going to eat?'

There was no point in taking the subject any further at present, she could agree with that, it was his manner of telling her to drop it that rankled a little. It would serve him right if she were still intent on the original aim, she thought wrathfully. No man was going to come the dominant male with her!

Her sense of the ridiculous came to the rescue, making her lips twitch as she looked across into steady green eyes. The militant feminist was hardly her style.

'Fifty-seven,' she said, 'with fried rice, please. Oh, and some prawn crackers to start.'

Whether he guessed what was amusing her or not, he made no comment, though his own face relaxed again. She had a sudden yearning to be alone with him, to have his arms about her, his mouth teasing her lips apart. Whatever his faults, he knew how to make love.

There was more to it than that, she acknowledged, fixing her attention on the glass in her hand. She was beginning to have a regard for him as a person—a friend. If Robert was telling the truth, and she had no reason to doubt it, then Dave had once been badly hurt by a girl he must have loved a great deal; his present avoidance of serious relationships probably stemmed from that same source. She didn't want to admit it, but the thought of being just another ship that passed in the night had the power to cause her rather more than a passing twinge. Emotional involvement was insidious; it crept up on one. Want it or not, she was caught in the net.

The estate where the Lyness family lived lay to the north of the city, nicely set out with red brick semis and maisonettes. Dave drew up in front of one of the former, pulling a face at the sight of the denuded young tree a few feet away along the pavement.

'If Jimmy had a hand in that I'll lay one on him!'

'Another brother?' asked Sara, getting out of the car.

'Eleven-year-old,' he acknowledged. 'And a rip! What doesn't . . .' He broke off as the front door of the house opened to emit a young boy with bright ginger hair who came racing full tilt down the path and through the gateless opening, putting out a hand to fend off the enthusiastic welcome. 'Hey, shouldn't you be in school?'

'Mom said I could stop home after dinner 'cos you were coming,' came the happy retort. 'I had yesterday off as well!'

'You'll not be able to do that when you move up to the comprehensive,' warned his brother. 'Not if you want to keep up with the rest.'

'Who's bothered about school!' The tone was derisory, the grin accompanying it lighting up the freckled, none-too-clean face. 'I bet you wagged it when you were there!'

'It isn't me we're talking about.' Dave's lips were twitching but he kept his face straight. 'Where's Mom?'

'Kitchen. She wasn't half mad when you didn't come yesterday!' For the first time he seemed to notice Sara still standing over by the car, sudden shyness clouding his cheeky features. 'I'll go an' tell her,' he added on a more subdued note, and shot back up the path again.

'I'd think she already knows,' Dave commented drily. He lifted expressive brows in Sara's direction. 'Ready?'

As I'll ever be, she thought. Smiling, she took the hand he held out to her and accompanied him up the path, trying not to dwell on the fact that the grass to either side was badly in need of a cut, the solitary flower-bed overgrown with weeds. Her own parents had never been interested in gardening as a pastime either; they had employed a gardener instead. Some people weren't so fortunate in having the means, although Dave should be well able to help out in that respect now. Always provided he wanted to do so, of course.

They went inside through the open front door. A square hallway gave access to the staircase and two other doors, both closed at present. Dave opened the one on the left to reveal a fair-sized kitchen lined with modern units and decorated in red and white. With her bright auburn hair and white blouse, the woman standing at the ironing board on the far side seemed almost to tone in with the general scheme. Dyed, Sara assessed with unerring feminine instinct, and not really suited to her skin colour—or what one could see of it beneath the layer of make-up. Fifty trying to look thirty was the initial impression. The cigarette dangling from the corner of her mouth did nothing to improve the image.

'I hope you've had your dinners,' she said without preamble, and without removing the cigarette, 'because I haven't got much in.'

'I told you we were eating first,' Dave rejoined mildly. 'This is Sara Mellor.'

Sara smiled at the other woman. 'Hallo.'

Appraising eyes skimmed the younger, shapelier figure with obvious envy. 'Nice costume,' she commented. 'Bet it cost you a few bob.'

'It wasn't cheap,' Sara acknowledged with a laugh, sensing Dave's reaction. 'I don't know about here, but clothes in London are a terrible price!'

'Always could tell a good cloth,' came the faintly complacent retort. 'Used to work in't rag trade.' This time the woman took the cigarette from her mouth, stubbing it out in a saucer on the nearby working surface. 'If you want a cup of tea you'd better put kettle on, Dave.'

'I think Sara would rather have coffee,' he said.

'No, I wouldn't,' she denied. 'Not always. A cup of tea sounds fine.'

'Have a seat,' invited Mrs Lyness, indicating the red formica-topped table with a nod of her head. 'Have to finish this lot now I've started it. I'm not gettin't board out again.'

'Dad at work?' Dave asked, filling the kettle at the sink as Sara pulled out a chair.

'He's on nights,' came the short reply. 'You know where to find him if you want him. He's never far away from them birds of his!'

'Pigeons,' advised Dave for Sara's benefit. 'He races pigeons.'

'Races 'em, breeds 'em, feeds 'em—even sleeps with the bloody things!' The tone was scoffing, derisory; Sara could see where both Robert and Jimmy got it from.

'Only once when his best hen was sick, and it can't have been a comfortable night,' Dave put in expressionlessly, dropping tea-bags into an earthen-ware pot.

'Serve him right,' came the judicious comment. 'And you're supposed to warm that before you put tea in.'

'I thought that only applied to loose tea.'

'Since when were you an expert then? You'd better stick to knocking balls about. You can do that all right.' She paused briefly, flicking her son a wounded glance. 'You ought to have come yesterday. Whole street was looking out for you. They had it on down at Club. You should have heard 'em! Just like VE night.'

'Glad you could get to see it,' he said.

'Oh, I only watched right at end. They had a good

turn on earlier.' There was a pause, a change of tone. 'I won on't Bingo again last week. Sixty quid! Nice to have a bit extra coming in.'

Something tensed momentarily in Dave's jawline, as if his teeth had come together, but his voice sounded normal enough. 'Good for you.' He finished pouring the boiling water into the teapot and replaced the lid. 'I'll take Dad a mug up.'

'Go and tell him to come down here for it,' advised his mother, 'else he might not get to meet your girlfriend. I don't suppose you'll be staying long.'

It was more of a statement than a question, Sara thought. Obviously they were not expected to stay. She resisted the impulse to offer help as Dave set out crockery on the sink-side. He seemed well capable of performing the task himself. Liking it was something else again judging from the wry tilt of his mouth when he brought a cup across to where she was sitting at the table.

He went out through a door at the rear of the kitchen, affording Sara a glimpse of a long, narrow garden with what looked like a couple of sheds at the end of it. The spring sunshine beckoned invitingly.

'It's a beautiful day,' she murmured, at a loss for something to say to the woman still busy at the ironing board.

'Yeah.' Pale brown eyes lifted to scan Sara's face again. 'You and our Dave known one another long then?'

'Only since Sunday night,' Sara admitted, then smiled. 'Or early Monday morning, to be exact. We were introduced at the party after the game.'

'Bit of a surprise him bringing you back here. Can't remember last time he brought a girl home. 'Course, he doesn't live here any more. Suppose you knew that already.'

'I know he has a flat the other side of the city,' Sara

said carefully, not about to let out that she had visited it herself. 'He left home a long time ago, didn't he?'

'Six or seven years. Not good enough for him, this place.'

'I'm sure that wasn't the reason.'

'You know him that well, do you?' She didn't wait for a reply. 'Don't know where he gets his ideas from! A right tearaway he used to be. Stole a motorbike once. Finished up in hospital.'

'Was he driving it?' asked Sara.

'No, one of his pals was. Made no difference in court. Dave got six months.'

Sara blinked. 'Prison?'

'Probation. Wouldn't have been prison anyway. He was only fifteen.'

The subject under discussion came back into the house, accompanied by a man with greying hair and a face that was an older replica of Dave's own. He was a couple of inches shorter than his son, and heavier, his stomach straining at the waistband of his trousers. Jimmy followed on behind, sidling sideways to plant himself in a corner where he could view proceedings without making himself the centre of attention.

'Hallo, luv,' said the father cheerfully to Sara without waiting for introductions. 'Nice to see a friend of our Dave's. How long are you here for?'

'They're not stopping,' put in his wife. 'They've got better things to do.'

'I meant here in Sheffield,' he retorted mildly, still looking to Sara. 'Dave said you're from down south.' He made it sound like a foreign country. 'Londoners don't usually think there's much going on in these parts—apart from't snooker.'

Sara was smiling, drawn by the man's easy manner. 'I'm not really a Londoner,' she denied, 'not by birth, at any rate. I lived in a village most of my life.'

'Squire's daughter, eh?' with a twinkle.

She laughed. 'Not quite. It's what they call a dormitory area. My father travelled up to town every day.'

Concern replaced the twinkle. 'Not dead, is he?'

'No,' she said levelly, 'my parents are divorced.'

'That's a shame.' He had taken a chair at right angles to her, his back to his wife. 'Some folks just can't get on.'

'Are you and our Dave going to get married?' demanded Jimmy suddenly, drowning out his mother's faint snort.

'We don't have any plans that way,' replied Sara, horribly aware of her face warming, and hardly daring to glance in Dave's direction.

'She's leaving tomorrow so we'd be a bit pushed,' said the latter, obviously amused. 'Fancying yourself as a pageboy?'

'No fear!'

He sounded just like Robert, Sara reflected, joining in the laughter produced by the indignant denial. He didn't look like him though. There was little resemblance to his mother either, apart from the hair, and that was hardly the same shade. It might have been once, she supposed—except for that skin tone. Mentally she shrugged. It hardly mattered.

'I hear you keep pigeons,' she said to the man opposite, and saw his eyes light up again.

'That's right. Would you like to see them?'

Out of the corner of her eye, Sara could see his wife's face. To say she was displeased would be a gross understatement, came the rueful thought. It was too late now to regret the inquiry, and beyond her to refuse the offer. 'I'd love to,' she said.

'Right.' Mr Lyness drained his mug, setting it down again with a thud as he pushed back his chair. 'You two stay and keep your mother company,' he said to his sons.

Outside, he led the way along the crumbling garden path, oblivious to any difficulties she might be having in her high heels. There were about a dozen birds on view through the wire netting fronting the first shed, with another dozen or so, she was assured, in the back. They all had names, some of them, like 'Big Bertha', very descriptive. Sara was allowed to hold one of the fantails, a lovely white creature which nestled without fear in her cupped palms.

'They're beautiful!' she exclaimed. 'Does Jimmy help you with them?'

'When he's not out getting up to mischief.'

She said lightly. 'He sounds a real pickle! A lot like Dave at his age, from what his mother was saying earlier.'

'Aye.' Subtly, the man's mood had altered. 'Something like.' He seemed to brood for a moment, watching the activity within the caged area. 'Dave's a good lad,' he announced unexpectedly. 'Wants to buy us a bungalow out in Derbyshire.'

'But you're not too keen?' Sara hazarded, reading between the lines.

'It's not a case of being keen, luv. It'd be grand living right out in't country with nobody to grumble about droppings and that when I fly this lot. I'm up for redundancy in a couple of months, and I'm not likely to get another job at my age, so there wouldn't be any trouble about getting to work or anything.'

'So it's Dave's mother who doesn't want to go?'

'Aye.' He sighed. 'She doesn't like leaving't Club, you see.'

'Perhaps she's worried about Jimmy's schooling too,' Sara ventured, trying to stay impartial.

'There's buses.' His tone was dismissive. 'Anyway, it's not coming off, so no use talking about it. Now, see that little 'un there . . .'

It was Sara who eventually suggested they return to

the house; not because she was bored, although pigeons, she privately thought, were not the most interesting of creatures, but because she was fairly sure Dave would be ready to leave.

She wasn't mistaken. The atmosphere in the kitchen was heavy, with both mother and eldest son too obviously on opposite sides of some fence. Jimmy had disappeared, but he put in an appearance again as the two of them went down the path to the car.

'Don't want to live in no country,' he muttered, kicking at a tuft of grass. 'Nuthin' to do!'

'I don't think you're going to have to worry about it,' his brother said on a grim note. 'You go into school tomorrow, you hear me?' He grinned suddenly, and ruffled the boy's hair. 'Here,' passing across a folded pound note, 'don't spend it on rubbish.'

'Some hopes,' he added ruefully as Jimmy shot off again with a whoop of delight. 'It'll be straight round to the local shops for comics and sweets!'

'If you wanted him to save it perhaps you should have given it to your mother to put in his piggy bank, or whatever,' Sara suggested mildly, and heard his short laugh.

'Sure I should!'

Not a good idea, Sara surmised, getting into her seat. She could sense they were being watched from the kitchen window, although the red and white flowered curtains didn't move. Mr Lyness had been genuinely sorry to see them go, but not his wife. She had barely spoken. With a mother who apparently lived for this Club they kept talking about and a father who only came to life when he was with his pigeons, it was small wonder that Dave had felt moved to get out on his own, she reflected. His offer to buy them a new home had fallen on stony ground, so far as mother and younger son were concerned, at any rate. Perhaps the former would simply prefer the money itself? Whichever, Sara felt in sympathy with Dave whose main concern was obviously with young Jimmy. He wanted for him all the things he had missed out on himself. Only he was fighting a losing battle, if she was any judge, because the pattern was already too well set.

'So what do we do with the rest of the day?' she queried, shelving the whole subject as they moved off from the kerb edge. 'It's only around four.'

'Two choices,' he returned. 'I can drop you back at your hotel and pick you up for dinner same as yesterday, or we can take a couple of steaks back to the flat and cook our own.' He paused, glancing her way briefly. 'We could even take a walk later on. The park's close enough.'

'I'm not dressed for walking,' Sara pointed out, lifting one of her feet in its high-heeled shoe.

'We can pick up some others on the way,' he came back reasonably.

She laughed. 'You don't really want to go out for a meal again at all, do you?'

'No,' he admitted. 'I've had enough of people for one day—present company excepted.'

Sara knew what he meant. She was feeling a bit that way herself. Being alone with him had its drawbacks too, but she couldn't bring herself to care overmuch about that aspect right now. After today she might never see him again. For all his talk of London not being the other end of the earth, it was unlikely that he was going to have much time for visiting, in the near future at least.

It took bare minutes to slip up to her room at the hotel and get the pumps she had worn the previous day. They were the wrong colour to go with her suit, but did it really matter? A stroll in the woods called for comfort above all.

They called in at a supermarket to collect the steaks and fresh salad ingredients, together with a punnet of early strawberries and a carton of cream. A bottle of Nuits St Georges completed the menu. A repast fit for a king, as Sara laughingly remarked. She felt in sparkling mood, her whole body alive and receptive. That it was all due to Dave, she could hardly deny. What she chose to ignore was the small warning voice at the back of her mind saying that no good would come of it.

Prepared between the two of them, the meal turned out to be one of the most enjoyable Sara had ever eaten. Afterwards Dave insisted they leave the dishes, and dragged her out into the evening sunshine. There was a spring-like coolness in the air still, but scarcely a breath of wind to stir the treetops. Strolling at his side along the path, Sara had a sense of well-being amounting almost to contentment. It was ages since she had walked anywhere apart from round the stores.

Others had elected to spend their time in the same way. Of the people they passed, only one man recognised Dave for who he was, and he contented himself with a cheery greeting and a thumbs-up sign.

'Wonder whether he was wishing me luck with the game or with you?' commented the recipient lightly when they were out of possible earshot.

'You pays your money and you takes your pick,' she responded, borrowing his tone. 'I've enjoyed these last two days, Dave.'

'This one isn't over yet.'

'To all intents and purposes it is. I'm taking an early train tomorrow so I don't want to be too late in tonight. I thought we might have a coffee when we get back, then you can take me back to the hotel.'

His shrug was philosophical. 'If that's what you want.'

It wasn't so much what she wanted as what was

going to be the safest bet, Sara acknowledged wryly. Dave was under her skin, his every touch a torment. She would have liked to be close again to that clean-limbed body, to have his mouth on hers, so warm and compelling, to fill her nostrils with his male scent and know that same indescribable sensation. No other man had ever reached that inner core; she hadn't fully realised her own potential to respond. And not just physically either. In two days she had come dangerously close to falling in love with a man who was probably the antithesis of everything she had once imagined so essential. The sooner she got away from him, the sooner she would come to her senses. She *had* to come to her senses!

Dusk was falling by the time they returned to the flat. Sara elected to make the coffee, a decision with which Dave was wholly in agreement. Seated side by side on the sofa, they watched the lights spring beyond the trees as darkness crept in, not bothering to switch on a lamp themselves because it was too much trouble. Sara herself was the first to stir, putting down her cup with a faint, regretful sigh.

'Time I wasn't here. I still have to pack my things.'

'That's hardly going to take you long,' Dave pointed out with some truth. He had his arms lifted, clasped hands comfortably supporting his neck, legs stretched. 'Anyway, you no more want to go than I want to take you.'

Her heart increased its beat, nerve and sinew tensing. 'There's confidence,' she said, 'and over-confidence. We already agreed we'd go right after coffee.'

'Noises,' he said. 'What you'd probably call a token gesture, if you were being honest with yourself.'

'Are you calling me a liar?' she demanded, and immediately felt ridiculous as she saw his mouth widen.

'I think the lesser word is prevarication. You knew

as well as I did where coming back here again was going to lead.' He put out a hand and rested it on her arm as she made to rise, not heavily but with enough firmness to stay her movement. 'Don't run away again. Not tonight.'

Her voice sounded husky. 'You think twenty-four hours make such a difference?'

'I think it's immaterial,' he said. 'It happened the minute we set eyes on each other, and we both knew it. If you walk away from it you'll always be wondering what you missed.'

'There's no future in it,' she murmured desperately, conscious of the gentle rubbing motion of his thumb against her skin.

'There doesn't have to be a future in it. Now is all that matters.'

'That from someone who spends his life thinking three moves or more ahead!' she scoffed, trying for a lighter note.

'Only when I'm playing.' The hand tautened a fraction, drawing her to him, his other hand coming out to caress the line of her cheek. 'I'm not playing now, Sara, not in any sense. I want you very much.'

Something inside her seemed to break open as his lips touched hers, releasing a surge of emotion too powerful to resist. She found herself kissing him back, feverishly, wantonly, not even attempting to hide the desire any more. Her blouse was undone, his hands on her breasts, but it wasn't enough. She needed to be with him, a part of him—to feel his heat and hardness possessing her.

It was Dave who made the move, getting to his feet and swinging her up in his arms. The bedroom was off the lobby. He made it without switching on any lights. laying her down on the soft duvet.

'No rush,' he murmured, coming down beside her. 'There's all the time in the world.'

She lost track of it completely after that, her consciousness limited to touch and taste and scent. He undressed her gradually, between kisses, managing at the same time to shed his own clothing. The moonlight angling in through the window cast a pearly sheen over his skin, outlining the muscular structure of his shoulders as he knelt above her.

'Relax,' he said softly when she stiffened a fraction at the intimacy of his hands. 'This is my party. All you have to do is enjoy it.'

'Lovemaking is supposed to be about give and take,' she whispered, allowing her body to melt again as it wanted to. 'I seem to be doing all the taking right now.'

His laugh came low, his lips brushing butterfly kisses across the soft, fluttering skin of her stomach. 'We'll redress the balance later. Just let go.'

She did because it was impossible not to, reaching climax after shuddering climax in the moments following. He left no stone unturned, no avenue unexplored in his efforts to discover what gave her pleasure. She had never realised just how many erogenous zones the body possessed until now, and he knew them all. Writhing, gasping, begging him to stop even while her hands clutched him closer, she was lost to everything but the moment. When he finally came inside her she was past all restraint, body moving with abandonment to the powerful thrusts of his loins until he collapsed across her with a strangled cry that echoed her own lost sound.

CHAPTER FIVE

THEY must both have fallen asleep almost immediately after, because when Sara opened her eyes again they were still in much the same position except that the bulk of Dave's weight had shifted a little to the side. How long they had slept, she had no idea. Long enough for her legs to become cramped at any rate, she thought wryly, easing them a fraction.

She froze as the man pinioning her stirred, then slowly relaxed again when he failed to waken. Ridiculous reaction anyway, she chided herself. After all he'd done to her, it was a bit late to start feeling self-conscious. Her stomach muscles contracted at the memory. How could she regret an experience like that? He had dominated her totally, and she had loved it. She could even find it in herself to want a repeat.

A smile touched her lips as she twisted her head to look into the part of his face not buried in the pillow. Redress the balance later, he had said. Well, why not? If she was going to regret this night at all she might as well do it wholesale.

The light run of her fingertips down the length of his spine brought him fully awake, although he didn't move at once. Sara put her lips to the point of his shoulder and kissed her way hungrily along it to reach the corner of his mouth, stifling a gasp as the arm still lying across her tautened to pull her closer. At the same time he rolled part way on to his back, his hand transferring to her nape in order to bring her mouth into line.

'My turn,' she reminded him between kisses, trying to keep a clear head. 'Redress the balance, you said.'

'You're already doing it,' he responded. 'I can't think of a better way to bring a man back to life!' His hands slid down her body to bring her all the way on top of him, a groan escaping his lips as her weight came to bear. 'God, you feel good!'

If the initiative had ever been hers it was lost to her now, she thought fleetingly as he fitted her to him, but the sensation was too exquisite for resentment to form. She closed her eyes, letting herself go, feeling his hands tauten about her hips as he exploded inside her.

This time they neither of them fell asleep afterwards. It was Sara who broke the satiated silence in the end to ask what time it was. Putting out a reluctant hand, Dave picked up the bedside clock and peered at the illuminated figures.

'Gone two-thirty,' he said.

That brought her head up. 'It can't be!'

'It is, though.' He pulled her down again, kissing her temple. 'There's no point getting het up about it now. We may as well settle down for the night. You can pick your things up in the morning.'

'And have them know I was out all night?' she objected, trying not to give way to the temptation. 'I don't have that kind of face.'

'Did you turn your key in when you fetched your shoes down?' he asked.

'Well, no,' she admitted. 'I was in such a hurry I didn't think about it.'

'Then nobody need know. You can slip in and pack your case, then check out as normal.' He added comfortably, 'You might have to catch a later train than you planned, but that shouldn't be too much hardship.'

'You mean,' she said with just the faintest edge, 'it's a small price to pay for what I've gained tonight?'

'Don't put words in my mouth,' he came back without apparent resentment. 'We both gained from tonight. One hell of a lot!' The pause was brief, the smile almost audible. 'Want to do it again?'

'Braggart,' she retorted, relinquishing any last lingering doubts. 'Pride goeth before a fall!'

'There's a lot in that,' he acknowledged. His voice softened as his arms drew her close. 'You're quite a girl, Sara.'

'You're not without merit yourself,' she murmured, drowning herself in his masculine scent. There was a pause before she added almost without volition, 'Do you think I'm easy?'

'Easy?' The surprise was not assumed.

She was already kicking herself mentally. The question had been so gauche. 'Anybody's for the asking,' she elucidated on a deliberately flippant note.

'If I'd thought that I wouldn't have been interested,' he said. 'There's no challenge where there's no contest.'

'Is that all it was, a challenge?'

The reply was a moment in coming. 'Would you rather I said I fell madly in love with you on sight?'

'Heaven forbid!' She forced a laugh. 'I never did believe in fairy tales.'

'That's okay then, I won't tell you any.' One hand was in her hair, the touch soothing. 'Is it essential you go back tomorrow?'

Some spirit of self-preservation drew the answer from her. 'Yes, I'm afraid so. Anyway, you can't escape your own commitments much longer.'

'That's true. I'm going to be in the bad books with the press as it is.'

Sara said slowly, 'You can't expect to escape publicity in your line. Not when you're winning.'

'Publicity I've no objection to, not where it concerns the game. It's this ferreting into the background I don't like.'

'But that's what people like to read about. It gives

everybody a boost to realise that you don't have to be
born with a silver spoon in your mouth to make a
success in life.'

The hand in her hair stopped moving. 'You've met
my mother,' he said after a moment. 'She'd be in her
element telling my life story to the press. Trouble is,
there's no knowing what she might let out once she got
going.'

'You mean she might tell them about your
probation, for one thing?'

'She obviously told you.' His tone was roughened.
'That wouldn't matter so much, it's on record
anyway.'

Sara kept her head down against his chest, feeling
the strong, steady beat of his heart at her cheek.
'There's something worse?'

'Depends how you look at it.' He sighed suddenly,
recommencing the slow caress. 'I saw you studying
young Jimmy this afternoon. What were you thinking?'

'Thinking?' She was puzzled. 'What was I supposed
to think?'

'That he doesn't look much like anybody else in the
family, for one thing.'

'Well, no, I don't suppose he does, if it comes to
that, but I still don't . . .' She broke off as the
thought suddenly came to her, the pause heavy with
innuendo. 'You're not just saying he's adopted, are
you?'

'No, I'm not. I'm saying there's a chap down at the
W.M.C. that he's the spitting image of, though.'

'I see.' She did, only too clearly. 'Does your father
know?'

'He's got to suspect. Not that he'd say anything.
The point is, I don't want Jimmy finding out.'

'But surely your mother would never . . .'

'I wouldn't take bets on it. His wife and her are

always at loggerheads. Sheer spite can do a lot of damage. Anyway, I'm not prepared to take any risks.'

Sara waited a moment or two before saying hesitantly, 'Are you sure you're not getting the whole thing out of proportion? I mean, even if anyone ever did find out, it's doubtful if they'd consider it worth a mention.'

'The man's a well-known local figure, not too well liked in some circles. There's plenty who'd use it against him.'

'I'm surprised you haven't gone after him yourself.'

'It's a bit too late. I only found out for sure about twelve months ago, though I'd had suspicions for years.'

Her head lifted. 'Your mother told you?'

'That's right. Retaliation because I was going on at her about not making Jimmy go to school. The only person she cares about is Number One!'

It was a dangerous thing to say under the circumstances, but the words were out before she could stop them. 'Perhaps she got tired of coming second to a bunch of pigeons.'

His body went taut. Abruptly he pushed her away, sitting up to shove a rough hand through his hair. 'What would you know about it? Dad might have his faults, but he was always a bloody good father!'

'Better than he was at being a husband, perhaps,' she retorted, sticking to her guns. 'I know all about men with other overriding interests. My own father was a case in point—although I imagine you might consider it perfectly natural for a *man* to indulge in extra-marital activity!'

The glance he turned on her was anything but lover-like. 'You're pushing your luck,' he growled. 'It wouldn't be the first time I'd tanned a woman's backside!'

'That I don't doubt!' For the first time in minutes

Sara became aware of her nudity. It took every ounce
of control she had to resist the urge to cover herself up
with the sheet. 'I suppose it's all part of your macho
image!'

There was a pregnant silence while they glared at
each other. It was Dave whose lips began suddenly to
twitch, the anger fading as humour caught up. 'We're
rowing like an old married couple,' he said. 'Let's call
it a draw.'

He could melt her so easily; she had already
discovered that. Now was no exception. Returning his
kiss, feeling his body springing to life again between
them, she could only be thankful for decisions
previously made. If she did see him again after today
there would have to come a time when the record must
be put right, but it wasn't going to be essential to tell
him what her original intention had been unless he
actually asked. One taste of his other side was enough
to last her a long time.

Waking in a strange bed with a man at her side was a
new experience. Dave was still out to the count, face
turned away from her, the duvet pushed down to waist
level. His back looked so smooth beneath its tan, the
muscle dormant. Beyond him, over by the window,
stood the sunbed he had spoken of, its canopy lowered
to create a curving cocoon. A smile touching her lips,
Sara wondered what it would be like making love with
the heat turned on—a thought which brought a swift
and surging arousal. Sheer gluttony, she told herself
wryly, and slid from the bed before she could give way
to temptation and wake Dave up. They had already
played that scene.

He came into the bathroom while she was drying
herself after a shower, a short dark robe belted about
his waist. His hair was tousled as if fingers had been
raked through it, his jawline rough.

'Early bird,' he commented, sliding his hands round under her arms to cup her breasts as he pressed a light kiss on the nape of her neck where the hair had parted. 'Mmmm, you taste good! Why didn't you wait for me?'

'I thought you needed your rest,' she said, stifling the urge to drop the towel and turn into his arms. 'Do you have a spare toothbrush?'

'No, but we can share.' He kissed her again, and released her, stepping away to open the wall cabinet over the sink and extract both brush and paste. 'Five minutes, then the bathroom's mine,' he warned. 'I already put the kettle on.'

Alone again for the moment, Sara squeezed toothpaste on to the brush and bent to her task, catching her own reflection through the mirror as she did so. Scrubbed and shining, she thought ruefully. At least she didn't look like a wanton!

She found it difficult to be as blasé about the affair as Dave himself had been just now. Obviously this wasn't the first time he had spent the whole night with a woman. The emotion that thought aroused needed no analysis: jealousy, pure and simple. Unwarranted considering the circumstances, but no less sharp for it. She would get over it, of course. She would have to. In the cold light of day, the whole relationship was doomed to failure. Her mistake had been in letting it get this far at all.

Putting on the same things she had worn all day yesterday was against her principles, but she had little choice. She would make sure she had time to change back at the hotel, she promised herself, even if it did mean catching a later train. Dave was leaning against the wall along the short corridor when she left the room, a glass of orange juice in one hand, the morning paper in the other.

'About the longest five minutes I ever knew,' he

observed, handing both items over to her in passing. 'There's ham and eggs in the fridge, if you're wondering.'

'I wasn't,' she said. 'I only want toast and coffee.'

'Do some for me then. Say ten minutes.'

He had vanished into the bathroom before she could form a reply, closing the door between them. You had your orders, she thought with humour, so get on with it!

Last night's dinner dishes still waited on the sink-side, the empty wine-bottle a mute reminder that drink was no bolster to willpower. Sara ignored them for the moment and concentrated on the breakfast, aware of a rising hunger as the smell of grilling ham permeated the air. On impulse, she added another slice. There was every possibility she might not get any lunch if the train she eventually caught didn't carry a restaurant car. She found herself enjoying the novelty in being here like this with the morning just under way, in setting up the breakfast bar for two and catching the sound of a cheerful masculine whistle as Dave moved from bathroom back to bedroom. Ten minutes, he had said; he still had three to go.

He came in just as she slid the succulent slices of ham on to two warmed plates.

'Changed your mind, I see,' he commented as she added fluffy scrambled egg. 'Sex obviously gives you an appetite.'

Sara felt her cheeks warm and refused to look up, aware of his amusement. In the light of day last night's activities took on a whole new aspect. Had that brazen creature really been her?

'I think there's a train around noon,' she said over a second cup of coffee. 'I can get a taxi down from the hotel.'

'I'll take you to the station,' he returned easily.

'But that's going to mean you hanging around while I get my things together and check out.'

'So? I'm not doing anything else this morning. Pity you're not staying a bit longer,' he added, 'I'm playing an exhibition match at a local scouts' club tonight. You might have enjoyed it.'

'I shouldn't have thought they could afford the world champion,' she said, avoiding the implied invitation.

'It was booked last year while I was still an up-and-coming. Not that it makes any difference.'

'Your agent would probably think so.'

'I don't have to do everything my agent tells me.'

'So I gathered the other night. You must be a sore trial to him, turning down all these lucrative offers.' She tagged on lightly, 'Do you think you'll ever change your mind about the commercial prospects?'

'Maybe. Depends how badly I needed the money. I did have this idea about starting a club for boys. Get some of them off the streets.'

'A snooker club?'

'What else? My probation officer got me interested, but it wasn't easy finding somewhere to practise. There's a wealth of untapped talent out there—kids who never had a chance to play on a full-sized table. Could be another Jimmy White just waiting to be discovered.'

Sara gave him a look of blue-eyed innocence. 'I suppose girls would be banned?'

'Discouraged,' he responded, undisturbed by the implication. 'They can play in their own league.'

'Pure sexual prejudice!' she accused.

'That's right. In some places women are definitely excess baggage.' His smile mocked. 'Leave us a few bastions of retreat!'

The sharp burr of the telephone cut across any reply she might have made. Dave reached over and lifted the kitchen extension, brows lifting as he glanced at the wall clock.

'Yes?' he said briefly. 'Morning to you too.' His eyes were on Sara. 'So I pulled the plug last night. R and R, the Yanks call it.' Another pause, and a change of tone, 'This week? Why not?' He listened a moment, mouth tilting. 'Just goes to show you should always keep on trying, old son!'

'I'll be coming down to London Friday,' he announced, replacing the receiver. 'Television chat show. You can show me the town.'

'Always assuming I'll be free that night,' she returned with a certain coolness.

Cynicism touched his mouth. 'If you want to be you can be. If there's any doubt, I'd as soon know now.'

There was discomfiture in her shrug. 'Not many women appreciate being taken for granted.'

'Not many women are capable of playing a straight game. I thought you might be one of the few.' The tone was brusque. 'No sweat, I can always come back home.'

'No!' The denial was torn from her. 'I'd like to see you again, Dave.'

'Okay, so let's take it from there.' He pulled forward pad and pencil. 'I'm going to need your address.'

She wrote it down for him, surprised to find her hand so steady. Friday was the day after tomorrow. Between then and now she had better find some way of explaining the misunderstanding over her job—unless she set out to clear all signs of it from the flat first, which was hardly practical. There was no doubt he was going to suspect her motives. What she had to do was convince him that his own stated feelings on the subject had stayed her hand. It was only the truth, after all.

She insisted on doing the washing-up before they left the flat; partly, she privately admitted, to alleviate the feeling of guilt because she hadn't been open with him from the first. He raised no objection. In all probability the dishes would still have been there Friday morning when his domestic help came in. She had to confess to an inner core of excitement at the thought of being with him again so soon. He would expect to stay the night, of course; she would be foolish to anticipate anything else. The affair was already under way—over-hasty in its inception, perhaps, but devastating in its enactment. How long it would last there was no way of knowing. She didn't want to think too far ahead.

They made the hotel for ten o'clock. As Dave had said, there was no problem. If any of the staff had taken note of her entry at all they would probably assume that she had been out to visit the shops. He waited for her in the covered car-park, getting out to take her suitcase and sling it in the boot when she eventually returned.

'Weighs a ton!' he remarked, eyeing her dark blue slacks suit as he slid into the driving-seat at her side. 'Do you always carry your whole wardrobe with you when you travel?'

'Just a fraction of it,' Sara acknowledged, and laughed. 'Clothes are my besetting sin!'

His eyes glinted. 'Not all the time.'

She felt her colour come up again, and was annoyed with herself. She was acting like a schoolgirl!

'A gentleman wouldn't have taken advantage of that opportunity,' she said with cool inflection, and saw his lips quirk.

'I'm sure you're right.'

Useless trying to put him down, came the rueful reflection as he started the engine. Words might arouse his anger but they couldn't undermine his masculine arrogance. Yet without that very quality, would she have felt the same draw? Other men she knew might treat her with more respect, but none had ever stimulated the same fascination.

It still wanted five minutes to train time when they reached the station, although it was already standing in. Dave left the car in the thirty-minute zone under the arches and accompanied her on to the platform.

'Should have known you'd be travelling first class,' he said drily when she had chosen a seat, glancing around the almost empty carriage. 'Waste of money if you're going to be spending most of the time in the restaurant car.'

'I had a good breakfast,' Sara responded, 'I doubt if I'll feel like any lunch.' Now that the moment of parting was here she wanted to get it over. 'You don't have to wait, Dave. We'll be off in a couple of minutes.'

'Come to the door, then,' he said.

She followed him meekly, letting down the window and leaning head and shoulders through to say smilingly, 'I feel as if we're filming another *Brief Encounter*!'

'Saw the remake on a plane a few years ago,' he acknowledged. 'Any man who could let Sophia Loren out of his clutches has to be a wimp!' He reached up both hands and seized her shoulders as the whistle sounded, drawing her down to press a brief, searing kiss on her lips. 'See you Friday.'

He stood where he was as the train began to move, a tall, lean figure of a man in blue jeans and roll-neck sweater. Sara wanted to put her hand over her mouth, to keep the feel of that kiss right there on her lips. Friday was going to be a long time coming.

Jeff Brady phoned on Thursday morning. 'So how did it go?' he asked without preamble.

'I decided not to bother,' Sara admitted. 'The interest would probably have been limited, anyway.'

'Depends on the market. I could have found you a home for it without any trouble.' The pause had a question mark wrapped up in it. 'It took you three days to reach that conclusion?'

'Two,' she corrected. 'I got back yesterday.'

'Hair-splitting.' His tone was a goad in itself. 'Methinks our Dave might have given you something else to think about.'

'Par for your course,' she said sweetly. 'Was there anything else?'

'Yes, how about dinner tomorrow night?'

'Sorry, I'm already booked.'

'Anyone I might know?'

'Do you move in Royal circles?'

He laughed. 'That Andrew sure gets around! Okay, I can take a hint. See you some time, beautiful.'

There had been no cause to be quite so biting, Sara reflected wryly as she replaced the receiver in its rest. Jeff meant no offence. There could even have been a time once when she might have responded to his particular brand of male charm, if on a minor level; only not while Dave was still in her bloodstream.

She had thought of little else in the past twenty-four hours, recalling the slow smile, the taunting glint in the green eyes, the certainty of his hands; remembering the things they had talked about, argued over, agreed upon. Hard of body and strong of mind, that was Dave Lyness. It was a devastating combination.

Friday brought a substantial cheque in payment for a series of articles on leisure activities she had sold to one of the leading magazines. The series had been fun to write because she had tried many of them for herself, including a couple of sessions at hang-gliding. She bought a bottle of Moët et Chandon in celebration, sticking it in the refrigerator for Dave's arrival. They could have a glass before they went out, she planned, and leave the rest for later—the thought of which sent frissons of anticipation up and down her spine. Enmeshing herself any deeper in this affair was

far from a wise move, but it was beyond her to turn
away from the encounter now. She had never wanted
anything more than she wanted to be in his arms
again.

On reflection, she had decided to leave explanations
for a while after all. She needed to know him better—
to have him know her better—before taking that risk.
The whole flat was tidier than it had been in months.
It looked, she had to admit, better for it. Furnished for
the most part in High-Tech design, it seemed cold and
almost clinical compared with Dave's place. She
doubted if he would think much of her taste.

At seven she switched on the television, sitting with
some impatience through a couple of interviews and a
musical interlude. Dave was on next, looking perfectly
at ease as he shook hands with the presenter and took
his seat. He was no stranger to either cameras or
audience, of course, Sara reminded herself. If he could
play a competitive game under their combined gazes,
he certainly wasn't going to be thrown by any studio
set-up.

He was wearing the same grey suit he had worn on
Monday night, she noted. There was every likelihood
that it was the only informal suit he possessed,
considering that so many of his evenings were spent in
dress uniform. He preferred casual clothes for every
day, that much she did know. Fleetingly she found
herself wondering how many other women watching
the programme right now knew how he looked
without any clothes at all?

The interview didn't last long. Taking into account
some of the questions asked and the answers given,
Sara wasn't too surprised. Dave was an expert at
parrying the cut-and-thrust, rousing the audience to
laughter on a couple of occasions with a ready riposte.
He received loud and prolonged applause on departure
from the set.

She was ready and waiting in simple black linen when the buzzer went at five minutes to eight. Dave's voice on the intercom sounded clipped and tinny. Sara took a swift glance in the lobby mirror while he was coming up to the second-floor flat, seeing her eyes sparkling like twin sapphires beneath the sideswept fringe of dark hair. In another moment he would be stepping through that door, mouth tilting as he looked at her, arms coming out to scoop her up against him. She could almost feel the crispness of his hair beneath her fingers, the vibrant masculinity of his body.

Expecting it though she was, the knock brought her heart into her throat. Taking a deep, steadying breath, she went to open the door, her carefully planned greeting fading on her lips as she looked into the taut features. Dave took her shoulder and spun her around to shove her roughly ahead of him as he came in and closed the door.

'We've got some talking to do, Miss bloody Mellor,' he said.

CHAPTER SIX

ALREADY suspecting the truth, Sara took refuge in an anger of her own when they reached the living-room.

'I'm not sure what this is all about,' she said shortly, spinning to confront him, 'but I'm not going to be pushed around by you or anyone else! Just say what you've got to say, then get out!'

Lips twisting, he tossed her the rolled magazine he was carrying. It was opened and turned back at an inner page. Sara scarcely needed to glance at it to know that her own name was blazoned there for all to see right under the article heading. Blue eyes met green without flinching.

'So?'

'That's you.' He was telling her, not asking. 'I checked with Jeff Brady this morning.'

Thank you, Jeff, she thought caustically, and knew she was being unfair. What else could the sports-writer have done but tell the truth? Dave would have found out anyway.

'Of course it's me,' she said. 'Good, isn't it? A first, I might add.'

'Rock star reveals all!' The tone was contemptuous. 'What did you do for *him* by way of persuasion?'

Her face flamed suddenly. 'It wasn't like that. It might have been at the very start, but I changed my mind.'

'Why?'

That question was one she was not ready to answer with any honesty. She chose sarcasm as a defence. 'Perhaps I decided there was nothing in your life and times worth writing about.'

'That's the attitude you'd better hang on to,' he clipped. His gaze slid the length of her, taking in the expensive cut of the little black dress, the slender line of her legs in their sheer dark stockings. 'Dressed to kill,' he added on the same hard note. 'You'd better get out of that yourself, I'd hate to tear it.'

Sara stared at him without moving. 'What are you talking about?'

'It should be obvious.' He was already removing his jacket, tossing it over the nearest chair and following it with his tie. 'You used me, I think I'm due to some recompense. I'd as soon take you to bed, but right here will do if that doesn't appeal.'

'Dave, stop this!' she jerked out, biting her lip as he unfastened shirt buttons. 'I didn't use you. You above anybody should know that!'

'You were good, I'll grant you. A real sex-kitten! You might even enjoy what's coming to you now if you let yourself.'

He was down to his belt, fingers flicking open the buckle. She said tautly. 'I'm not going to demean myself by struggling with you, that's for sure! If you're so intent on having your petty revenge, I'd as soon we used the bedroom too.'

If she had been hoping for any retreat on his part she was to be disappointed. He simply shrugged. 'Lead the way.'

It was necessary to pass him in order to reach the lobby again. She did it with head held high, but he made no attempt to touch her. Only when she was in the bedroom, with the brass bedstead and pristine white overthrow right there in front of her eyes, did the icy disdain start to give way. She had anticipated such a different atmosphere for this moment, relaxed from the champagne, yet stimulated by it too: both of them eager and ready to renew the intimacy so much enjoyed. She had been on the brink of something wonderful with this man now standing at her back.

'Get your things off,' he said harshly, 'unless you'd rather I did it for you.'

'If you're trying to degrade me . . .' she began.

'You already did that for yourself.' There was no softening of intent. 'With me, and how many others?'

It was a rhetorical question and she knew it, but she answered anyway, turning to look directly at him. 'I'm not in the habit of selling myself!' she said fiercely. 'If I'd still had any interest at all in doing a write-up on you I'd have made sure nothing happened between us!'

'Sure you would. And I suppose that drummer you did such a job on opened up for you when he wouldn't open up for anybody else just because he liked your face?'

'Or perhaps because I happened to catch him at a time when he was feeling a little publicity wouldn't do him any harm.'

'So he gave you the go-ahead to print all the lurid details.'

'As a matter of fact, yes. He even saw a copy before publication.' Her eyes gave off sparks. 'He liked the way I'd handled the material, if it's of any interest. If you thought what I used was lurid, you should have heard some of the stuff he *did* tell me!'

Dave shook his head impatiently. 'Don't try wriggling out of it that way, because it won't work. You conned me every inch of the way.'

'And *that*'s what it's really all about, isn't it?' she flashed. 'Macho man can't take a dint in his precious pride!'

His eyes were slitted, dangerous, devoid of any trace of humour. 'You might be able to talk to the wimps down here any way you want but you're not doing it with me!' he stated.

'I imagine any man who treats a woman with courtesy and decency would be a wimp in your estimation.' Her laugh was meant to deride. 'Well, let me tell you, David darling, that given a choice, *any* woman worth a damn would rather take her chances with a wimp than be swallowed up whole by a blustering walrus!'

He moved fast, pushing her backwards on to the bed. For a moment he towered over her, murder in his eyes, then the anger gave way suddenly to disgust—as much self-directed, she thought, as at her. When he rolled her over on to her face she was already half anticipating what was coming. Not that it made it any less painful in the event. He didn't hold back one iota.

It took her several minutes after he had slammed from the room to recover from the initial shock. The slaps had hurt and were hurting still, spurring the rage mounting in her. Who the hell did he think he was?

He had gone, of course. That was some consolation. It would serve him right if she brought charges against him. Assault was punishable by law. Except that describing the nature of the offence would prove more embarrassing for her than for him, she was bound to concede. The best thing she could do was forget both incident and man, as of now!

The fury lasted until she was on her feet and viewing her heated reflection in the dressing-table mirror. Only then did other emotions begin to emerge. Dave was gone, and he wouldn't be back. So much for all her plans, her anticipation. In that respect if in no other, it served her right for placing too much importance on what was after all just a sordid little affair. He'd taken all she had to offer and given her nothing in return—except abuse. She was well out of it; well rid. From now on she was going to stay in her own environment.

She took off the black dress and got into a lightweight wrap, feeling anything but happy. The champagne was still in the fridge, and it could stay there. A lonely celebration was no compensation. She would make herself some coffee and listen to Radio Four until it was time to go to bed. Or she could do some work on her current project. Anything rather than sit thinking about what might have been.

The sight of Dave sitting in the chrome and leather chair furthest from the living-room door brought total disconcertment. For a long moment she could only stand and stare at him. He was wearing his shirt again, but tie and jacket still lay where he had tossed them. He returned her gaze quite calmly, if unsmilingly.

'I thought you'd gone,' was all she could think of to say.

'I almost did,' he said, 'but then I decided we both needed time to cool down.'

'Fine.' Faced with a lack of any hint of apology in his tone, Sara felt the anger stir to life once more. 'So now we have, you know where the door is!'

Very faintly his lips twitched. 'Isn't that what you'd call a contradiction in terms?'

'Don't try getting at me that way either,' she snapped. 'You've already had your satisfaction!'

'Some, maybe.' He held up a hand as she made to speak. 'You asked for worse, and on balance I thought you'd prefer the hiding. And I'm not going until we straighten a few more things out, so why don't you sit down and stop carping.'

She made no move, breathing hard as she tried to regain some command. 'There's nothing to talk about. You made your opinion plain enough.'

'I wasn't in any mood to listen right then. I am now.'

Sara shook her head. 'I've done all the explaining I'm going to do. You didn't believe me then, there's no reason you should believe me now. Anyway, it isn't important.'

'No?' His voice had softened a fraction. 'Look me in the eye and tell me that, and I might believe it.'

For a brief moment she managed to do the former, but the words refused to come. Biting her lip, she said huskily, 'Pointless, then.'

'That remains to be seen.' He stretched out a hand 'Come over here.'

He was still doing it, she thought wrathfully, but found herself obeying anyway. He took her hand when she reached him, drawing her down on to his knees. His mouth was firm and warm and compelling, both demanding and gaining response. She was being a fool, Sara told herself, even as her lips refuted the argument. She should have finished it while she had the chance.

Dave was smiling when he lifted his head. 'That's better,' he said. 'Now we're back on an even keel.' There was a slight pause before he added a little gruffly, 'Sorry if I misjudged you. I wasn't thinking any too straight when I got here.'

'My fault,' Sara claimed. 'I should have told you the truth from the start.'

'If you had we wouldn't have had anything.'

'But we wouldn't have known what we were missing, so it wouldn't have reckoned.'

'There's something in that.' Dave kissed her again, lighter this time, and added humorously, 'I can't make love on an empty stomach.'

'You were going to,' she pointed out.

'I was mad enough to ignore the pangs. Anyway, I didn't intend taking much time over it.'

'That sounds like rape.'

'Near enough.' He sat up straight, bringing her with him. 'I'm not kidding, I go weak at the knees when I'm hungry, and I didn't eat since noon. How long will it take you to get ready again?'

'Too long,' she acknowledged. 'I could rustle you

up a meal of sorts right here, if you're willing to settle for something simple.'

'Any potatoes?'

'Well, yes, there might be a couple. I don't often eat . . .'

'Chips,' he said. 'With anything else going.' His grin made Sara feel weak at the knees. 'I could eat a whole horse!'

He almost did. Watching him devour the contents of the piled plate half an hour later, she could only wonder how he stayed in trim.

'Exercise,' he acknowledged when she asked. 'I work out three times a week at a gym. Plus a fast metabolism, I'm told.'

'Lucky you.'

'You don't need to worry,' he said, pushing the empty plate away. 'A few pounds wouldn't do you any harm.'

'You prefer fat women?' she queried with faint asperity.

'Voluptuous,' he corrected. 'Most men do. Child-bearing hips and big, luscious breasts, that's the ideal!'

'You should have lived in Rubens' day,' she retorted, aware of being teased. There was a pause before she added lightly, 'Do you think you might have children of your own one day?'

'Hadn't thought about it, but I expect so.' He studied her a moment, expression not easy to define. 'How about you? Are you a dedicated career woman?'

'Right now I am,' she admitted. 'I'm not sure about the future.'

'Well, at your age there's plenty of time.'

'Listen to the old man of thirty!' she taunted. 'One foot in the grave already!'

The glint springing in the green eyes refuted that suggestion. 'We'll leave the washing-up till morning,' he said. 'You just talked yourself into an early night!'

If it had been good between them before, it was even better this time. More so, Sara thought, because they had come so close to losing it all. Arrogant, chauvinistic and totally infuriating he might be, but she was in love with the man. She knew that for a fact. Held in his arms, feeling his body a part of hers, she wanted for nothing. It didn't even matter at the time that he might not share her depth of emotion. They were together, and that was all that mattered.

Morning brought a whole new perspective. On Monday Dave was due in Prestatyn. Between then and now he had to get back home and fit in at least a couple of extended practice sessions. It was important, he said, for the champion to keep on winning in order to set up a mental barrier between himself and the other players. Creating the illusion of being unbeatable was halfway to becoming it.

'So when do we see each other again?' Sara asked when he was almost ready to leave for his train, half hoping he would suggest she join him in the coming week.

'Hard to say for sure,' he admitted. 'Maybe next weekend, if nothing crops up between times.'

'And I'm supposed to just wait around on the chance that it doesn't?'

Dave sighed. 'Don't start that again. If you want to make other plans, then go ahead.'

She gazed at him, trying to veil the hurt she knew must be in her eyes. 'It wouldn't bother you if I saw someone else?'

'Of course it would bother me,' he growled, 'but you're a free agent.'

'As you are.'

'As I am.' He studied her for a moment before moving suddenly to take her by both arms and force her to look at him. 'Sara, we're neither of us ready for any kind of commitment. It's too soon, for one thing.'

And the same difficulties existed, she acknowledged. Before last night she would have agreed with every word, but before last night she hadn't fully realised what it was to be in love. Nothing else seemed as important as that.

'It's not even a remote possibility,' she agreed, letting pride take over. 'We'd do nothing but fight!'

'One way or another.' His thumb smoothed the line of her lips, making her ache for a more intimate touch, the slow smile almost finishing her. 'Could be worth it at that.'

How she stopped herself from clinging too hard when he kissed her she never knew. From somewhere she even found the will to break it off and step away from him. 'You'll miss your train.'

'There are others,' he said, but he went anyway.

The days following were not easy. Sara had never known time hang so heavily on her hands. By Thursday morning she was able to ascertain that Dave had won the professional championship, but was still no wiser as to when he might be expected to leave the camp. She kept the weekend free anyway, calling herself a fool for doing it but unable to bring herself to run the risk of missing him if he called. Had anyone told her even a bare two weeks ago that she would ever find herself in this state over a man she wouldn't have believed it, she thought wryly more than once. Love hadn't been on her agenda.

He came on the Saturday afternoon and stayed over until Sunday. They spent the evening dining and dancing, returning to the flat in the early hours to make love with a frenzy that left them both exhausted and replete.

'I've missed you,' Dave murmured in the aftermath when the world had stopped spinning and her bones had turned to water. 'You lost me the Open.'

'Conceding thirty points a frame can't have helped any,' she rejoined in an attmept to retain some measure of perspective, and felt the laugh start deep inside him.

'You know too much.'

Not about the things that mattered, she thought. Not about what went on inside this man's head. There had been a time way back when she had felt in charge of the relationship, but not any more; Dave held her physically and emotionally in thrall. When he spoke again she didn't quite take it in at first.

'Come with me to Vegas,' he said.

Her stillness brought his head up from the pillow, one brow lifting quizzically as he looked down into her face. 'Does the silence mean no?'

'It means,' she got out, 'that it's an awfully long way!'

'A few hours by plane, and only for a week.'

'What about the distraction?'

'It's mostly exhibition work—stuff I can do standing on my head. There'll be plenty of time for other things.'

The temptation was great. Her mind swiftly assessed the possibilities. There was nothing pressing on her calendar; nothing, certainly, that couldn't wait a week. Las Vegas with Dave. Seven whole nights even if she had to share the days. Could she bear to turn down that kind of opportunity?

'On one condition,' she said. 'I pay my own way.'

His eyes narrowed a fraction. 'Why?'

'Because that way I keep my independence.'

'Can you afford it?'

'Yes.' It would probably take a good proportion of her available capital, she calculated, but it would be worth it.

Dave rolled away on to his back, lying silently for a moment or two. When he did speak it was on a decisive note. 'We'll compromise. We can use some of the time between games to start drafting that book we once talked about. That makes you tax deductible.'

'You weren't serious,' she objected. 'We both knew it.'

'So I changed my mind.'

'In a week?'

'A lot can happen in a week.' He rolled back on to his side to look at her, one hand coming up to follow lightly the curve of her body from breast to thigh. 'You either come my way or not at all. It's up to you.'

With the tumult he could rouse in her threatening to overcome all bounds of control, there was only one answer Sara could make. As a compromise, the offer was still distinctly one-sided, but it was at least a step in the right direction.

They met at Heathrow an hour before the flight was due to be called. Dave eyed Sara's solitary suitcase with unconcealed amusement.

'Glad to see you took what I said to heart.'

'It made sense,' she admitted, 'thought it wasn't easy to decide what not to bring.'

His tone matched the dry little smile. 'A lot of the time you're not going to be needing clothes!'

That she could imagine. Dave was not a man to let opportunity slip through his fingers. Sara tried to convince herself that the ends always justified the means, and knew she only partially succeeded. This wasn't the way she would have wanted it if she'd been able to arrange things herself. Only she hadn't, and this was what she had got, so she was going to make the most of it. Later could take care of itself.

On the face of it he had not been joking about the book. They spent a good part of the journey assembling material. The technical detail would be down to Dave himself, of course, but it would be up to her to put it into easily readable form. For the rest, he said, she was going to need to take time out to follow him around the circuits this next season and gather some atmosphere.

'What about background?' she asked at that point, attempting to ignore the long-term implication in the knowledge that business and personal commitments had to be regarded in a totally different light. 'Obviously we shan't be doing more than gloss over your early years, but readers will expect something about origins.'

'Provided you keep Jimmy out of it,' he said, 'you can tell it any way you like. Come to that, Maureen wouldn't be too keen either. At least, her husband wouldn't.'

Sara glanced at him. He had his head back comfortably against the seat rest, eyes closed. 'Maureen?' she queried.

'My sister. Married out of her class. James is a company director, and they live in Baslow.'

'I *hate* that phrase!' Sara exclaimed emphatically, and saw his eyes come open.

'It's a fact of life. She adjusted fast enough. I suppose you could say she always did have grand ideas. A stuck-up little madam, my mother always called her.'

'And you agreed with her?'

'Never thought that much about it. She's a couple of years younger than I am. She was James's secretary.' A fleeting smile crossed the lean features. 'The wedding must have been sheer hell for him and his family. Not that they showed it, too well-bred. Mom turned up in a bright red mini-dress with a neckline nearly down to her navel. You might have gathered red's her favourite colour.'

Sara said softly, 'I think you're as big a snob in your own way as you're making your sister's in-laws out to be.'

'I didn't say they were snobs,' he denied, unmoved by the criticism. 'And I'm just a realist. Families like mine and James's don't have a lot in common.'

'How do you and he get on?'

'Reasonably well. I spend a couple of hours with them from time to time. It was Maureen who recognised your name—or I should say, she remarked on the coincidence. She takes just about every magazine on the market.'

Sara slanted another glance. 'What did you tell her about me?'

'Nothing. She called in home a couple of days after we were there.'

She wondered fleetingly what his mother had said about her, and decided it was of no consequence anyway. His family meant nothing to her.

It was evening when they landed, but the temperature was still in the upper seventies. Gazing out of the cab window as they drove along the famous Strip, Sara could scarcely credit the sheer spectacle. One hotel was built in the shape of a huge circus tent, with all the trimmings. Even though it was still daylight, the neon signs were already lit, creating a kaleidoscope of colour. So far there were relatively few people on the sidewalks.

Their hotel covered a whole city block, rising fifteen storeys into the hot desert air. To reach the elevators after checking in at the desk, it was necessary to thread one's way between massed ranks of fruit machines. At many of them stood people feeding in coin after coin, the movement synchronised with the long pull on the handle. The noise was ceaseless.

They were booked into adjoining rooms on the twelfth floor. Opening up the communicating doors, they stood together at the floor-to-ceiling window looking out over the lower buildings opposite to a desert springing into twinkling life as darkness fell. There were dwellings out there where there had seemed to be only sand. Far below lay the glittering ribbon that was the Strip, lined with opulent hotels, with casinos, with all the pageantry one might crave—and all designed with the express purpose of extracting dollars.

Sara drew in a long, slow breath. 'It's fantasy land,' she said. 'It reminds me a bit of that place Pinocchio almost finished up in.'

'Where they all turned into donkeys?' Dave laughed. 'You might have a point. Tonight's free. What would you like to do first?'

'Shower and change, and then eat,' she returned. 'And see Caesar's Palace, if we have time.'

'We have all night,' he said. 'I don't start work until tomorrow afternoon, so we can always lie in.'

'With all that out there waiting!' Smiling, she shook her head. 'We have to realise your childhood ambition.'

'Already organised. We're taking one of the tours by plane through the Canyon itself. Wednesday I'm free till the evening sessions. We can hire a car and drive out to Death Valley. It's only a couple of hours from here.'

Being with him at all would be the bonus, she thought. There were going to be times this coming week, she knew, when she was going to feel lonely. It was the price she had to pay for the rest.

She wore a trouser-suit in creamy-white jersey silk for the evening's foray. Dave himself donned pale slacks and a smart but casual shirt, the collar open on tanned flesh. Having seen the pool-room pallor of other players, she could understand his desire for a healthier look. The tan extended the full length of his body, apart from one small patch in the slight hollow at the base of his spine where the rays apparently couldn't reach. One sure way of telling the difference, he had said with that lazy smile of his; an opportunity not afforded to all.

In retrospect, the evening was exhausting. At the time it seemed purely exhilarating. They began with dinner in the hotel itself, choosing from a menu almost two feet long.

'I still have a bottle of this stuff waiting back home,' Sara observed, sipping the champagne Dave had ordered. 'It was supposed to be opened the night you did the TV show.'

'We'll have to find another excuse,' he said. 'It shouldn't be too difficult.'

His name was up in lights over one of the inner halls, billing him as 'King of The Snooker Table'. Only until somebody else came up with all the right breaks, was the cynical comment. Next year the title would remain the same but the name could well be different.

Outside the heat was tempered by a cooling breeze coming in from the desert. They walked the few blocks to sumptuous Caesar's Palace with its great sweep of forecourt drive and cascading fountains. White-jacketed attendants greeted arriving limousines. Apart from the Romanesque names over the various casino areas and showrooms, and the mini-togas worn by the cocktail waitresses, there was little to suggest ancient Rome, but it was plush. Acres of red velvet carpet stretched in all directions.

By sheer luck, they were able to secure a couple of cancellations for one of the top-name shows, sitting through two hours of glittering entertainment in the shape of dancers, magicians and singers for fifteen minutes of a brilliant comedian/impressionist who had only recently become well known in Britain. The girls were all long-legged beauties, the costumes lavish in design and scanty in content. A scenic feast, Sara privately thought, that could soon pall.

She was thankful to return at last to the air-conditioned quietness and privacy of their rooms, melting into Dave's ready arms the moment the door was closed. There was no question, of course, of occupying separate beds. The only choice they had to make was which of four King Size they should share. Lying safe, secure and blissfully content later, Sara made a mental note to rumple one of her own beds in the morning before the maids did the room. Just a gesture, she knew, but one she couldn't bring herself to forgo. Cohabitation was one thing, advertising it another.

Looking into the familiar sleeping features, she felt her heart contract from sheer weight of emotion. She loved this man so desperately; to contemplate losing him was agony, yet there was nothing permanent about the relationship. Even if the affair should extend itself to any length of time, there were going to be whole weeks when she wouldn't even see him. Could she take that kind of situation for long anyway?

CHAPTER SEVEN

DURING that week following, Sara had many opportunities to ask herself a similar question. No matter how masterfully executed, when one had watched the same trick shots set up a few times they tended to become commonplace. She preferred it when a challenge match was played, because it provided the opportunity to further her knowledge of the game in writing down each sequence of shots. She even drew diagrams to show the path each ball had taken. Worth saving for future reference, was Dave's gratifying reaction, but it didn't stop eventual boredom from setting in.

She was surprised to find how many women attended the sessions, both afternoon and evening. Some of them she would have thought too young to appreciate the finer points of the game at all. It was only when on one occasion she found herself seated in front of a couple of bubbly blonde teenagers that she realised the attraction might not be quite all it appeared. 'Poppy was right,' commented one to the other in a stage whisper. 'He *does* look like Clint Eastwood!' Dave grinned when she told him. He had youth on his side, he said.

The flight through the Grand Canyon was a stupendous experience. No photograph or film could convey the awe-inspiring contours of that great, branching rift in the earth's crust. The colours alone surpassed belief—all the hues of the rainbow etched in rock and stone. Flying within the mile-deep cliffs was both terrifying and uplifting at one and the same time.

'I'd like to come back and make that trip,' said Dave

when they spotted the two big black rafts on the river far below. 'I think it takes a couple of weeks to do the whole distance.'

Rather him than her, reflected Sara, looking down at the turbulent waters through the binoculars provided. Adventure holidays were not her scene. All the same, if he asked her she supposed she'd do it. Not that it was likely to happen. His immediate future was already fully booked.

Death Valley took her breath away in more ways than the one. With a temperature touching 110 degrees in the shade, and the air so dry that perspiration didn't even have chance to damp the skin surface, it was no place to wander far from the car. Just a few weeks before, she learned at the café-cum-museum close by the Grapevine Canyon entrance, a man had died of thirst when his car broke down after he had detoured from the mapped roads. Coloured signposts depicting a car full of skeletons were a timely if grisly reminder of what could happen to the traveller who ignored all advice and strayed from the beaten track.

By Saturday, Sara for one was more than ready for home. She spent the afternoon out at the pool, diving in every few minutes in order to keep relatively cool. Most of her fellow bathers were women and children. The men, she supposed, were all indoors gambling. It was, after all, what the majority were here for.

So far she had fed no more than a couple of dollars into the fruit machines, and that only in passing. Gambling was a mug's game, Dave had declared at the outset. The only tables he was interested in playing were those where the odds were even to begin. Coming down again from her room after a shower and change into cool white linen, Sara yielded to temptation and slipped a coin into a slot, watching the spinning symbols with self-derisory smile on her face.

The ringing bells, flashing lights and sudden clatter of
silver falling into the tray beneath brought an instant
crowd of onlookers, some frankly and unashamedly
envious, most cheering and clapping as Sara scooped
the jackpot into the roomy canvas and leather holdall
she was using as a handbag. There must be about two
hundred and fifty dollars, she calculated, laughing at
the good-natured banter. Not a fortune by Vegas
standards, perhaps, but a fair return on a quarter!
Wages of sin, Dave would probably call it. She could
hardly wait to tell him.

The session would be finished, she realised,
catching a glimpse of her watch. He might already be
upstairs getting showered and changed himself. She
turned back towards the elevators, flicking a casual
glance into the nearby bar area as she moved. The
sight of Dave perched on one of the tall stools talking
animatedly with a blonde-haired and stunningly
beautiful young woman brought her to an abrupt halt.

He was too intent on his companion to notice her
standing there, that was obvious. The girl was
laughing now, head thrown back to reveal a long and
lovely throat. Seeing Dave's slow smile, the familiar
flick of an eyebrow, Sara forced her limbs into
movement again, unable to take the swift, fierce
backlash of emotion. Damn him! She thought
painfully. Damn him, *damn* him!

The strap of her bag gave way just as she reached
the bedroom. She dropped it on the floor inside the
door and left it there. With the inner drapes drawn to
filter the sunlight, it was pleasantly dim. Sitting on the
edge of the bed, Sara eyed her reflection in the long
mirror set into the opposite wall and attempted to
come to terms with her battered ego. She had no false
modesty regarding the quality of her own looks, but
there was no way she could compete with that
showgirl out there. She wasn't even going to try. If

Dave was so bored with her that he needed to seek out other women, then let him have them!

She was packing when the knock came on the communicating door some twenty minutes or so later. Stonily, she went to open it, turning back immediately into the room to continue her task. Dave followed her in, watching her for a few seconds without speaking. She could sense the moment when initial puzzlement gave way to irritation.

'Okay,' he said at length, 'what's the beef?'

'I see you're picking up the vernacular too,' she retorted shortly. 'That must have impressed your new friend!'

'Oh, for God's sake!' He shoved an impatient hand through his hair. 'I bought the girl a drink, that's all.'

'From the way you were looking at her, thirst-quenching was certainly in your mind!'

'Like an open book to you, is it?' The tone derided. 'We've come a long way in three weeks.'

'Not far enough so it can't stop right here,' she flashed, straightening from the suitcase. 'I'll pay back every penny you've spent on me if you'll let me have the bill. Less tax, of course. You can hardly claim it from more than one source.'

'You've a real way with words,' he said after a tense moment of silence. His voice was soft, almost silky, his mouth set in lines she knew only too well. 'I'm not going to try taking you on in a slanging match. There's a better way of fetching you down off that soapbox of yours!'

'We've already played this scene,' she reminded him tartly, refusing to back away as he moved towards her.

'No, we didn't.' The grey eyes held a dangerous light. 'That time you got me side-tracked. This time you won't.'

His hands were hard on her arms, lifting her bodily from the floor to toss her down on to the bed. He came on top of her before she could move, weight pinning her, taking her breath. There was no shred of tenderness in his mouth, in the hard thrust of his tongue between her clenched lips. Only when her body stopped rejecting him and began answering his demands did his attitude undergo any change; even then the anger still came through.

It was Sara herself who made the first move towards reconciliation, taking his face between both hands to kiss him long and despairingly on the lips.

'I hate you,' she whispered. 'You know that, don't you?'

'The same way I hate you,' he responded with the faintest of smiles. He studied her face, expression slowly firming, as if he had come to some kind of decision. His move to get up was purposeful. 'Get dressed,' he said. 'We're going downtown.'

She came up on an elbow, uncertain yet of his mood. 'What for?'

The answer came like a bolt from the blue. 'To buy a ring initially. We're getting married.'

Shock rendered Sara speechless for whole seconds. When she did finally find her voice again it sounded odd even to her own ears. 'You're joking, of course.'

'No, I'm not.' Dave tucked his shirt into his waistband, meeting her eyes with undiminished resolve. 'They don't call this place the wedding capital of the world for nothing. There's no blood test, no waiting period. We get the licence, say the words, and that's it.'

Sara said dazedly, 'How do you know so much about it?'

'I saw it in a guide book.'

He came back to the bed, leaning down with both hands planted either side of her to brush her lips with his in the manner he knew drove her crazy, holding her there suspended as her body tensed to the fresh surge of desire. When he straightened again she was lost, and he knew that too. It was there in his eyes, in his smile, in the way in which he held out a hand to help her to her feet.

'Get dressed,' he repeated, 'I have to be back for the first session. Tonight's my final appearance.'

The white cotton was too crumpled to wear again. She chose a blue one instead, fingers nerveless as she pulled down the slim skirt. She was going to be married to Dave. It didn't seem possible. Yet she wanted it. Oh, *how* she wanted it! Just the two of them together!

It all happened so fast. There was the trip downtown by cab, the purchasing of a single gold band, the businesslike atmosphere at the County Courthouse. They weren't alone in the deed. There were others tying the same knot, one couple so young they looked fresh out of school. Then it was back to the hotel and a quick meal before Dave had to leave her.

Watching him play that evening, she felt the pride of possession. That's my husband, she wanted to tell those around her—especially the women. He was the same man in bed that night. The difference was in her. Sara Mellor was no more. Mrs David Lyness had taken her place. It felt good.

They were on the plane going home before the practicalities of the situation began to raise problems. He was playing the following night, Dave stated, so they would need to make the call to pick up whatever was necessary very brief. Her affairs would have to be sorted out gradually, he added. She would need to give notice over the flat, anyway, so there was no particular rush.

It was the first time it had even occurred to Sara that she might be expected to move north, lock, stock and barrel. To say the idea held little appeal would be an understatement, she acknowledged ruefully, feeling her heart take a sudden plunge. Marry in haste, repent at leisure, wasn't that what they said? Not that she regretted marrying Dave. Of course she didn't. She was crazy about the man.

Crazy, came the fleeting thought, was probably the operative word!

'We can keep the flat as a *pied à terre*,' she suggested, trying to be reasonable. 'After all, we can well afford it between us.'

'We don't need it,' he said.

She gave him a swift glance, keeping her voice down because people around them were sleeping. 'You're not proposing I should give up my job?'

'No, I'm not.' He hadn't turned his head. 'But you're freelance. You can do the same work from anywhere.'

'It doesn't work like that. I have contacts.'

'The telephone was invented some time ago.'

'There's no call for sarcasm,' she retorted. 'I'm trying to find a compromise. I haven't asked you to move down to London.'

'There wouldn't be much point,' he agreed. 'Anyway, aren't you forgetting you'll be working on the book?'

She drew in a long, slow breath, aware of the anger and resentment building up inside. 'I don't want to fight about it,' she said with control, 'but you have to see that you're being unfair.'

'In taking it for granted that my wife is going to live with me in our own home?' He was looking at her now, mouth set. 'We're going to buy a house and put down some roots, Sara. I'll want to know you'll be there when I come home to it.'

'With your pipe in one hand and your slippers in the other, I suppose!'

Unexpectedly his lips twitched. 'Smoking isn't one of my vices.'

She knew what was. How *well* she knew! Mind fought with matter, gaining little ground in the process. She had married Dave of her own free will; she had to make some attempt at least to come to terms.

'All right,' she murmured reluctantly, 'we'll try it.'

He reached for her hand. 'That's my girl!'

His girl, his wife, his bedmate. And what else? came the thought. Not once had he said the words 'I love you'. Not once. But then neither had she, if it came to that. There had been times when she had been on the verge, yet she hadn't followed through. She didn't want to be the first, she supposed, if she really got down to it. Yet one of them had to be. Provided Dave even felt the same kind of emotion where she was concerned. How could she be sure?

It was raining and chilly when they landed. Tired after a sleepless night, Sara could only hope the weather wasn't an omen for the future. Never had the flat seemed more inviting, more secure. Standing in the doorway, looking round at all the items gathered over the past two years, she wondered how she was going to bring herself to start sorting out what to keep and what to get rid of. Certainly it was going to take longer than a few hours. Her clothes alone would take up a trunk.

'It's impossible,' she said out loud on a note of despair. 'It's going to take me at least twenty-four hours to even make a start.'

'We don't have twenty-four hours,' Dave pointed out. 'Just throw a few things in a case for now and leave the rest for later. The furniture isn't yours, is it?'

'Some of it.' Sara spread her hands in a helpless little gesture. 'It isn't just that. There are a thousand and one things I need to see to. I can't just leave it all in the air, Dave. You have to see that.'

He was silent for a moment, studying her, expression difficult to read with any accuracy. 'You know I have to be back in Sheffield tonight,' he said. 'What's the solution?'

'I'll stay over for a couple of days and get everything sorted,' she came back quickly. 'Then I can come north with a clear mind.'

'A couple of days? I thought you said twenty-four hours just now.'

'I said *at least*. Forty-eight would be better. I'd be with you by Wednesday at the latest.'

He said drily, 'I think I'd better quit while I'm ahead.'

'Then you don't mind?'

'Of course I mind.' His voice roughened a fraction. 'It's a case of needs must. I'm not dragging you on the train by the hair!'

Perversely, she almost wished he would insist on her accompanying him here and now. The thought of three whole nights away from him was depressing. Yet she needed the breathing-space too, they both did. There was more to marriage than a simple change of name; it called for a whole new attitude to life.

In the end Dave caught the noon train, after eating an early-lunch-cum-late-breakfast at a fast-food bar *en route* to the station. He refused to allow Sara on to the platform with him, kissing her goodbye on the forecourt surrounded by jostling crowds of damp travellers.

'I didn't expect to be leaving you again so soon,' he acknowledged wryly. 'Just make sure you're on this same train Wednesday.'

'I'll be there,' she promised, resisting the urge to cling to him now that the moment of parting had come. 'It's better this way, Dave, you'll see.'

'I'll take your word for it.' He kissed her again, briefly this time, and was gone through the barrier.

Those two days were in some ways the shortest and in others the longest Sara had ever spent. She missed Dave, she was bound to admit. Not just physically but emotionally too. She tried phoning him a couple of times, but without success; whether because he was genuinely out or simply not answering the telephone she couldn't begin to guess. The fact that he made no attempt to reach her, even though she left the answering machine on night and day, hurt more than she was willing to acknowledge. She had no right to blame him under the circumstances, she knew, but she did even so. She so desperately needed to hear his voice, to have him say the few words which might make her forget about everything else. If this was his way of punishing her for her unwillingness to drop everything for his sake, then he was succeeding. Yet she refused to be sorry for it either. Some kind of stand had been essential.

Jeff Brady was one of the few people she told about her change in status. His reaction was all she might have anticipated.

'You'll never make a go of it,' he stated bluntly over dinner that Tuesday evening. 'An affair is one thing, but marriage!' He paused, shaking his head. 'What possessed you, Sara?'

'I love him,' she said, trying to carry conviction. 'Isn't that enough?'

'Not nearly, even if it's true. You must realise the adjustments are all going to have to come from your side?'

'Not all,' she denied. 'Dave made a major contribution in leaving me down here at all.'

'Bet it's the only one,' came the shrewd observation. 'Once you join him up there you'll be in his world. I can't see it ever being yours.' He eyed her for a moment across the dimly lit table. 'Are you giving up the flat?'

Sara hesitated before answering that one. 'I'm supposed to be.'

'But wisely you've decided to hold your horses. Going to tell him?'

'Of course.' She added quickly, 'I'm going to need a little time to get all my things sorted out, in any case. I've used up this last couple of days just dealing with the paper work. Bank, tax office, passport, to name but a few.'

'You'd have been better off leaving well alone till you saw how things were going to develop. There's no legal requirement for a woman to use her husband's name.'

'Maybe not, but I couldn't see Dave taking very kindly to having a wife named Miss Mellor,' she responded with a faintly wry smile. 'At least no one can say I didn't make the effort.'

'Hope it's appreciated, then—though I doubt if it will be.'

Sara doubted it too. It would probably not even occur to Dave that she would consider doing anything else. The decision to reserve giving notice on the flat for some future date had not been arrived at lightly; she knew he wasn't going to like it. All the same, burning all her bridges at one and the same time was too drastic a move. She had to have some fall-back just in case.

'You should have married me,' said Jeff on a note not meant to be taken seriously. 'We'd have stood more chance than you do with Lyness.'

Except that I don't love you, she thought, hiding her reaction behind a laugh and a light rejoinder. Except that your touch can't set me alight the way Dave's can! She knew a swift, overwhelming surge of longing to see the man she had married—a flaming of passion only he could ease. At that moment everything else seemed insignificant.

He was waiting for her on the platform when she arrived Wednesday afternoon. Sara went into his arms like a homing pigeon, oblivious to other alighting passengers.

'You were so sure I'd be on this train?' she queried half jokingly, when the first flush had been appeased.

'I was sure of one thing,' he said. 'I'd have been on the next train down if you hadn't turned up.' He lifted an eyebrow at the two suitcases. 'Don't tell me this is all you've brought?'

'The rest is coming,' she promised. 'I've enough here till it arrives.' She fell into step at his side as he hoisted the bags, slanting a glance to refresh her memory of the lean features. 'What have you been doing with yourself these last few days?'

'Not a lot,' he said, 'apart from a couple of exhibitions.'

'But you haven't been home very much.'

It was Dave's turn to slant a glance. 'Is that a question or a statement?'

She tried to make the shrug nonchalant. 'I phoned a couple of times, that's all.'

'Obviously the wrong times.' They had reached the top of the steps, their footsteps sounding hollow on the bare boards of the covered bridge. 'I was at my sister's most of yesterday.'

'You told her about us?'

'Any reason why I should keep it a secret?'

'No,' she said, 'of course not.' Her pause was brief 'How did she take it?'

'She's reserving opinion till she's met you. We're going out there for dinner tonight.'

Sara bit her lip. 'You might have given me a bit more time.'

'For what? You've already met the rest of the family.'

'Not as your wife.'

'No.' He grinned. 'Jimmy was relieved he didn't have to get dressed up for another wedding. Not that he can remember all that much about the last one.'

'And your mother?'

The smile disappeared. 'The least said the better. We'll just have to prove her wrong.'

It didn't take all that much imagination to guess what had been said. Sara only hoped Dave's faith was not unfounded.

Driving through the city, she found it difficult to realise that it was only a little over four weeks since her very first visit. So much had happened so fast! Too fast. She had always intended to be at least twenty-eight before she considered marrying anyone, if she did it at all. Her own parents still had to be informed. How her father might react was difficult to assess. These days she hardly knew him. Her mother would no doubt be devastated; not that she would have wanted all the trouble of a conventional wedding, Sara was reasonably certain. Her life was far too full to allow much time for parental duties. Perhaps as well considering what Dave had said about Maureen's wedding. Her mother would never have recovered from the embarrassment.

It was a relief in many ways to reach the flat and close the door and be alone with Dave again. His kiss was lingering, dispelling any doubts she might have been harbouring regarding his feelings for her—physically at least. She felt the familiar rising excitement, the need to press herself close against his hardness. When he turned her in the direction of the bedroom it was what she wanted too, more than anything in the world.

Broad daylight or not, he made no attempt to draw the curtains. Sara delighted in the hunger she saw in his eyes as he looked at her, trembling to the touch of his hands. Three days were scarcely long enough to have forgotten anything about his lovemaking, yet it was almost like the first time again in the sheer quality of discovery. He knew her so well, bringing her again and again to the very point of climax before finally granting her release into shuddering ecstasy.

Lying under him, thigh muscles still trembling from that ultimate spasm, she ran loving, tender fingers down his spine.

'I didn't realise how starved I was,' she whispered.

'Up here starved means cold,' he returned softly. 'You're far from that!'

'You don't give a girl much option.'

'I don't intend to either.' His face was buried in her hair, his voice muffled. 'It's been a long three days.'

'For me too.'

'You could have shortened them.'

'I had too much to do.'

'So I gathered.' His lips nuzzled her neck. 'All taken care of?'

Now was not the time to be telling the entire truth, and Sara knew a very good way of distracting his attention. She heard him catch his breath and felt his immediate response, meeting his lips halfway as passion flared swiftly again between them. Later, when the moment was right, she would tell him about the flat. Or then again, maybe she wouldn't. A few days weren't going to make any difference when it came to giving notice.

They drove out to Baslow via the same route they had taken that very first day. Maureen and her husband lived in a large, ivy-covered house off the main thoroughfare. Dark-haired and attractive, the former greeted her brother's new wife with some reservation. James was older than Sara had anticipated by some ten years, his fair hair thinning on top. He shook hands formally when introduced.

There were no other guests at dinner. Seated in the

oak-beamed dining-room, Sara looked out on extensive lawns stretching down to a stream, the view beyond it of wooded hillside.

'You live in a lovely place,' she commented. 'It's difficult sometimes to realise just how close the city really is.'

'People moving up here when the Midland Bank transferred its Head Office had the same surprise,' said James. 'Plus property prices being a whole lot lower into the bargain. I reckon this place would fetch another fifty thousand down south.' His glance shifted to Dave on the other side of the table. 'Still thinking of buying out here?'

'Mom doesn't fancy it,' Maureen put in quickly. 'I already told you that.'

'I meant for himself,' returned her husband.

'Derbyshire for certain,' Dave acknowledged. 'Hope Valley for preference. Sara will be doing most of the looking.'

Blue eyes lifted swiftly. 'I will?'

'There's not much point in both of us trekking around. 'When you find something you like I'll take a look.'

'And make the ultimate decision?'

'We'll do that together.'

'You're going to find it very different from London,' James put in a little obviously. 'We make our own entertainment. Maureen is an excellent cook so we give a lot of dinner parties.'

Sara's smile was bland. 'I doubt if my culinary expertise will impress anyone. Perhaps we can hire someone to do it for me.'

'I know a woman who will come to the house and take over the kitchen for the evening,' said Maureen, taking the suggestion at face value. 'She's very good too. All you have to do is decide on the menu.'

'We're getting a bit far ahead, aren't we?' Dave

sounded amused. 'How are the twins?'

'Fine.' To Sara, she added, 'They're both in bed, of course. They always go at seven.'

'Of course.' It was apparent that Maureen was taking it for granted Dave would have filled her in on detail such as sex and age. She tagged on lamely, 'I'll look forward to seeing them another time.'

'You might have warned me about the children,' she said later when they were in the car heading homewards again. 'I could have made all the right noises.'

'Didn't think about it,' Dave admitted. There was a pause before he added casually, 'Like kids, do you?'

'I've never had very much to do with them. Fine in small doses, I imagine.'

'You'll feel different when you get some of your own.'

She shot him a glance, senses responding as usual to the hard-edged profile. 'Do I take that as a statement of intent?'

He laughed. 'Right on, babe!' Something in her silence reached him, drawing his own swift glance. 'It's a part of the contract.'

'Yours maybe, not mine. Not without discussion first.'

'I can hardly do it without you.'

'I'm not joking!' she flashed. 'I don't want children.'

His face went blank. 'Not ever?'

'I don't know about that. Certainly not for a few years, anyway?'

'You're only twenty-three now. There's time enough.'

'Provided I produce to order when you decide?'

'Hey!' His voice was soft, the inflection not. 'Let's not make an issue of it.'

'We have to,' Sara insisted. 'It's one of the things

we didn't give ourselves time to think about. I'm not
sure I'm cut out for motherhood.'

'Practice makes perfect.'

Her hand came down hard on the seat arm between
them. 'Will you stop treating this as some kind of
female contrariness! I have as much right to my
feelings on the subject as you have to yours!'

'All right.' He was obviously making an effort to
retain his temper. 'So we shelve it for another time.'

'That won't solve anything.'

The car came to a sudden, screeching halt at the
roadside, jerking her forward against the restraining
belt. Dave made no move to switch off the engine, face
austere in the moonlight as he looked at her.

'All right,' he said again, 'let's have it out here and
now. I told you I wanted to put down roots.'

'I know what you told me.' She was shaken, her
emotions confused. 'That's all you've ever done—tell
me!'

'If that's true, it didn't stop you marrying me.'

'So I made a mistake.' She saw his expression alter
and knew a swift rejection of that statement, but the
words wouldn't come. The mistake had been in timing
as much as intent. They should have waited, talked it
through when they were both of them in a fit state of
mind to see the pitfalls. A marriage based almost
purely on lust stood little chance of lasting. She didn't
love Dave; at least not in the way she should. If she
loved him she would want his children—wouldn't she?

'I'm beginning to think we both made a mistake,' he
said after a lengthy pause. 'I saw you differently.'

'We don't even know each other.' Her voice
sounded husky. 'Dave, it isn't going to work. Not this
way.'

'What other way did you have in mind? Me
commuting to London between matches?'

She hadn't got as far as that, and it was hardly

meant as a serious suggestion, but she seized on it
anyway, the way a drowning man might clutch at a
straw. 'It doesn't have to be that one-sided. Other
people manage to find a workable arrangement.'

'We're not other people. This is between you and
me, nobody else.' His tone was brusque. 'If you don't
want a house of your own just yet, okay. We can keep
on the flat. Only I'm not having a wife living a couple
of hundred miles away. If it's change you want, you
can always travel round with me.'

'Watching you knock the same old balls round the
table! No thanks. I already exhausted the enthusiasm.'
She caught herself up there, ashamed of the outburst.
Her hand went out impulsively to touch his sleeve in
a gesture of apology. 'I didn't mean that.'

'I think you did,' he said expressionlessly, 'but it
isn't vital. I don't find what you do for a living all that
riveting.' His face was turned to the front, eyes fixed
on the darkened landscape just visible through the
windscreen. He seemed to be considering his next
words. When he did speak again it was on a measured
note. 'You were right about one thing. We only know
one another in bed. So we'll start from there. Given a
few weeks, we might get to sort things out.'

Given a lifetime, she thought hollowly, they would
never sort *this* out. They were light-years apart in
almost everything essential to a partnership. She could
find no reply. None, at least, that added to anything
already said.

The rest of the journey was accomplished in silence
from both sides. Sara had unpacked what clothes she
had brought with her earlier. It left her with nothing
to do but prepare for bed. Dave made no attempt to
share the bathroom with her the way they had been
accustomed to doing in the past. Coming out, she
thought she heard the clink of glass against glass from
the living-room. He didn't normally indulge in a

nightcap. Tonight he obviously felt the need. Sara could have done with a bracer herself, if it came to that. Not that alcohol was going to solve any problems. All it was likely to do was blur them a little.

She was in bed but far from sleep when he finally came through. She stiffened when he slid into bed and reached for her, resentment flaring anew. 'Is this your answer to everything?' she demanded fiercely.

'Not altogether,' he said, 'but it helps.'

Evading the issue, she thought as he found her mouth. The problems would still be there in the morning. It made little difference, she had to admit. Her mind might say one thing, but her body still reacted the same.

CHAPTER EIGHT

SHE opened her eyes again on daylight, imagining herself back in her own flat for a moment of two. The sound of movement drew her head round on the pillow. Dave was already up and dressed. He finished tying his shoe-lace before coming over to the bed to bend and kiss her lightly on the lips.

'Practice,' he said succinctly. 'We're taking a team out to Australia ten days from now.'

'Is this something new?' Sara asked, trying to bring her mind into sharper focus. 'Or did you already know about it?'

'It's been put together since the championship,' he admitted.

'How long for?'

'Couple of weeks. Too good to miss even if it did mean using a shoe-horn to fit it in.' His smile was fleeting. 'It's going to be a hectic schedule, but you'd get to see quite a bit of the country. Fancy it?'

She said slowly, 'Are any of the other players taking wives along with them?'

'Could be. Haven't asked.' He straightened again. 'Anyway, think about it. I'll see you around midday. I thought we might go find you a car this afternoon. You're going to need transport of your own. Decide where you want to eat lunch.'

Knowing the possibilities might be a help, she thought caustically as he left the room. She heard him pick up his cue-case from the lobby, then the closing of the outer door. Moments later an engine sprang to life in the road below. Only when the sound had diminished to a faint drone did she finally stir herself into action.

The face she saw in the bathroom mirror showed distinct signs of a heavy night, her mouth still slightly swollen and tender, her eyes retaining the memory of moments too volcanic to be extinguished at will. Man couldn't live on cream alone, she told herself cynically. The daily bread was an essential factor. Dave had not intended asking her to accompany him on the Australian tour, she was fairly certain. He had probably anticipated that she would utilise the time looking at houses. When it came right down to it, the game meant far more to him than she did—than any woman ever could. A wife was someone to come home to, he had said it himself. Even today, knowing how she felt, he had made no attempt to stay with her and try to sort things out. If this was to be the pattern of her days, the nights would hardly be adequate compensation.

The unexpectedly early delivery of her trunk gave her something else to think about. She unpacked only the items she considered essential, telling herself storage space was too limited to bother with the rest. With the furnishings rearranged to accommodate her typewriter on a small table by the window, and her books occupying the top two shelves of the nearby bookcase, there was still no sense of permanency. She felt positively homesick for familiar surroundings, for the ever-present sound of city traffic, for the friends and acquaintances who were just a phone-call away. They were, she supposed, still only a phone-call away, but it was hardly the same thing.

When the telephone rang around eleven, she almost ignored it. The call was sure to be for Dave anyway. Only when the tone had sounded a dozen times or more did she finally and resignedly lift the receiver.

'This is Beryl Morton from the ground-floor flat,' announced a pleasant female voice. 'I thought as Dave wasn't back yet, you might like to come on down for coffee?'

About to refuse, Sara suddenly changed her mind. Being unsociable wasn't going to help. 'Thanks,' she said. 'I'll be right there.'

The other met her at the door. She was in her early thirties, Sara judged, tall and elegant in the lightweight Jaeger suit. Her mid-brown hair was beautifully styled.

'I just got in from the hairdresser's,' she acknowledged, interpreting Sara's glance. 'I'm normally at work at this hour, but we're going to a dinner-dance tonight so I took the day off. I saw Dave earlier when I was fetching the milk in.'

'Did he suggest you ask me down?' queried Sara, following her hostess through to a living-room the same overall size as the one upstairs, though far more modern in décor.

'Oh, no, that was my own idea,' Beryl waved a hand in the direction of a curved chesterfield. 'Sit down. I'll just get the tray.'

Sara wasn't at all certain what it was she wanted to hear. A request by Dave would at least have shown some concern. She wondered just how much these neighbours of his knew about their relationship.

Beryl enlightened her on that particular point almost immediately. 'I must say,' she said, pouring the coffee, 'it was a surprise when Dave told us he was married. I suppose you wanted to escape all the publicity.'

'Something like that,' Sara agreed.

'Of course, we haven't known him all that long,' continued the other. 'He only moved in upstairs just before Christmas. They're nice big flats, aren't they?'

Sara couldn't argue with that. 'Very. Have you lived here long yourselves?'

'About five years. It's a nice area, and handy for town as well. John and I run a computer advisory service. It's hectic, but tremendously worthwhile.'

'You must both be brilliant,' Sara observed in genuine admiration.

Beryl laughed. 'I understand computers; it doesn't follow I'm good at everything. John is the real brains of the outfit. He writes his own programmes.' She offered the plate of biscuits. 'Dave said you were a journalist. Shall you be trying for a job on the local paper?'

'I doubt it. I'm freelance.'

'Oh, I see! Well, I'm sure they'd welcome the odd article. I know the editor if you'd like an introduction.'

'I'm fine at the moment, thanks,' Sara said swiftly, trying to feel properly grateful for the kindness. 'If I get stuck it might be an idea.' She changed the subject. 'Do you do the gardening yourselves?'

'Mostly me. John isn't much interested in gardening. Feel free to take advantage of it any time you want. It gets plenty of sun and it's very private.'

She would hardly be sunbathing in the nude, came the tart thought, followed at once by faint shame. Beryl was simply trying to make her feel at home. It wasn't her fault that the chances were remote.

She left about a quarter to twelve, and Dave arrived some twenty minutes later. 'Had a good morning?' he asked, selecting a clean shirt from the drawer in the bedroom prior to taking a shower.

'My trunk arrived, and I had coffee with Beryl from downstairs,' acknowledged Sara from the dressing-table stool where she was putting the finishing touches to her eye make-up. 'The time simply flew!'

'Good.' If he had noted the gibe he wasn't reacting. 'Do you have any idea which car you'd like to drive?'

'I hadn't thought about it,' she admitted, pushing the mascara wand back into its case. 'Where am I supposed to be driving, anyway?'

'Wherever you need to. I realise it's only the country's fourth or fifth largest city, but I don't see you running round it on the bus.'

Sara didn't see herself running round it at all. She wondered if Dave would expect her to visit his family. Of them all, Maureen and her husband were the only ones with whom she felt any kind of rapport. Once they had got off the subject of houses and homemaking, the evening had proved a fair success. Perhaps if she had been a few years older the thought of settling down to bring up a family of her own might have had more appeal; there were so many things she still wanted to do.

'You choose for me,' she suggested. 'I don't really mind provided it goes.'

'Fair enough.' If her lack of interest irked him in any way he was keeping it to himself. 'The new Renault had a good write-up.'

She said in surprise, 'You're talking about buying new?'

His brows lifted quizzically. 'You'd rather have a beat-up old wreck?'

'Well, no, of course not. It's just ...' She paused irresolutely, not even certain why she was hesitant. On impulse, she got up and went to him, sliding both arms about his shoulders to kiss him full and hard on the lips. 'You're too generous, Dave,' she murmured.

'Start that, and we're not going to get out of here before teatime,' he growled softly, clasping her waist as he kissed her back. 'If I didn't have this great gaping hole where my stomach should be I'd say to hell with it!'

'I suppose a conscientious wife would have got up and made you a proper breakfast before you left this morning,' she said with a hint of asperity.

'Only if she had some warning. Which reminds me, I'm booked for an exhibition at a youth club the other side of town tonight. Are you going to come and support me?'

With the only alternative an evening alone right

here in the flat, there was little real choice, Sara reflected drily. 'Another pre-championship booking?' she asked out loud.

'No, this one's purely a private arrangement, for a friend.'

So easily cancelled or postponed, she thought, and knew she was being unreasonable. 'Yes, of course I'll come,' she said.

They ate at a local Berni Inn, then spent an hour or so taking a test drive. Sara had learned to drive as soon as she was eligible, but had never actually owned a car before. Even with her name on the papers, she didn't feel she owned this one either, not with Dave writing the cheque. They were promised delivery the following morning when insurance formalities were completed.

With the exhibition due to start at seven, and a twenty-minute journey to get there, it was a case of making do with a hastily contrived meal out of what was in stock. Sara promised herself a shopping expedition as soon as she got the car. Cooking wasn't by any means her favourite occupation, but she felt bound to make some effort towards playing the dutiful wife. It was the long-term prospect she found depressing.

The youth club met in an old disused Methodist chapel on the city's east side. Run by a couple Dave's age who were both qualified teachers, it offered a place where teenagers could get together and play games or records, even dance if they felt like it. A makeshift bar served soft drinks and crisps.

Sara was surprised to find so many attending, particularly the small group of punk enthusiasts with their cockatoo hairstyles and studded denims. Not regular members, confided the female half of the club leadership, whose name was Julie.

'I hope they're here out of pure curiosity and not for

trouble,' she added with a wry intonation. 'We don't refuse anyone entry, but it could cause problems if two factions decided to use the premises as a battlefield. The girls are the worst. They egg them on.' A smile widened her lips as she glanced across the room to where Dave stood surrounded. 'Not that they're any of them above a bit of hero-worship on occasion. You can't believe what it's done for our image, getting the world champion to come and show them how it's done. I only hope the table is going to be all right for him. It was a throw-out from a club they were pulling down, so it's seen some action—to say nothing of what it gets here.'

'He'll manage,' said Sara. 'I daresay he's played on worse.'

'Not for a long time, though.' The other gave her a sideways glance. 'You're a southerner, aren't you?'

All the way through, Sara thought. 'It's all the same country,' she said lightly, still watching the group across the room. 'I think we're going to start.'

The exhibition followed a predictable pattern, starting with the Triangle shot where a cue ball was made to jump over fifteen reds and through an upended frame-rack, and finishing with the spectacular Grand National in which seven balls were bounced in fast succession off three cushions to leap the butts of cues laid end on to the pocket. Bad table or not, Dave made no mistakes. He also managed to keep up a patter that had the majority of his audience hanging on to every word. When invited at the end to try their own hands at the same trick shots, they were by no means reticent in coming forward.

Watching, Sara could only wonder at the patience Dave displayed as he lined up the balls time and time again and set the would-be player on the right track. He got along well with young people, it was easy to see. They responded to him. Probably, she thought, because he treated them all, no matter what age, as equals.

'This has to be one of the most trouble-free nights we've had this year,' Julie commented gratefully over a glass of orange juice.

'It isn't over yet,' warned her husband, raising his voice to make himself heard above the sudden blare of sound from the tape deck. 'Let's get the doors closed before we start counting chickens!'

'Why do you do it?' asked Sara. 'I mean, teaching all day, and then this.'

Bob grinned and shrugged. 'Gluttons for punishment, I suppose.'

'They're two of the dedicated ones,' said Dave in the car going home. 'Little enough thanks they get for it most of the time. The finance comes mainly out of their own pockets.'

'Apart from the contributions you make,' hazarded Sara. 'You do, don't you?'

'Some,' he admitted. 'They're worth helping.'

'I can see why you're so keen on that snooker club idea,' she went on thoughtfully. 'There were one or two in there tonight even I could see had talent.'

'That's right. They're self-taught for the most part too. The only tables they normally get to practise on are in pubs.'

'I'd have thought they were mostly under age.'

'They are.' There was a pause. When he spoke again it was on a different note. 'Feeling better about things tonight?'

'Yes,' she said, and told herself it was only half a lie. She had to give it a chance.

It was the following Tuesday before the press latched on to the news. The first Sara knew of it was when a local reporter turned up at the door asking for verification. Heard it in a pub the previous night, he said when she asked him where the information had come from. Was it true she was a newspaper-woman herself? There was no point in prevarication. Sara gave him the bare details, thankful for once that Dave himself wasn't around. She would have time to warn him before anyone got to him.

Reaching him by telephone proved more difficult than she had anticipated. Joe Walker was reluctant to interrupt his client's game. Only when Sara said crisply to tell him it was his wife speaking did she get her own way, and that only because he was in shock.

Dave sounded amused when he came on the line. 'You just ruined all Joe's illusions,' he said. 'He doesn't think women are all that good for a man's concentration, much less wives! Nothing wrong, is there?' He listened to what she had to say, his shrug almost visible. 'I suppose it had to come out some time. No real reason why it shouldn't. Still, I'm glad you let me know. I'll be ready. See you in a couple of hours.'

So what had she expected? Sara asked herself as she returned the receiver to its rest. So far as Dave was concerned, the marriage was no particular secret. She was the one reluctant to acknowledge her status.

Mrs Shipley, the domestic help, brought two brimming cups through from the kitchen, which she was giving what she called a 'good bottoming'. 'I made us a nice cup of tea, love,' she said, setting down her burden on the dining-table. 'Come and get it now, before it goes cold.'

Sara complied, hardly liking to mention that she preferred coffee to tea at the best of times, and always in a morning. Mrs Shipley came in Tuesdays and Fridays, and kept the whole flat sparklingly clean. Dave had not suggested any change in the arrangement, and Sara herself had no desire to take over the woman's duties. She had managed to keep her own place surface-tidy, but rarely found time for more than a run over with vacuum and duster. There was more to life than domestic chores anyway. Different for Mrs Shipley who was being paid for it.

'Did you tell anyone about Dave and me?' she asked, sipping resolutely at the hot tea.

'Only Jack,' came the comfortable reply. 'A real fan, he is! Followed Dave—Mr Lyness—since he got started.'

'If you've always called him by his first name there's no reason to stop on my account,' Sara advised. 'What does your husband do?'

'He's cellarman up at Mucky Duck. Black Swan, love,' she added kindly, anticipating the comment already forming on Sara's lips. 'Keep forgetting you don't come from round here. I suppose you'll be looking for a proper house now you're married, like. They're nice flats, these, but they're only meant for a couple. If you stay on this side of town I'd still be able to come and do for you.'

'We haven't really got round to deciding anything just yet,' murmured Sara evasively, 'but I'll bear it in mind.'

'Right.' The other heaved herself to her feet. 'Got to get on. Work won't do itself.'

She took her own cup and saucer back to the kitchen with her, leaving Sara to contemplate the strong brown liquid still half filling hers. Heard in a pub, the young reporter had said. It certainly seemed to fit. Not that she could lay any blame at the Shipleys' door. How were they to know how she felt about it when she didn't even understand herself? The best she could hope for was that none of the nationals would pick up the item. She needed time to adjust to being Mrs Dave Lyness herself before it became wide knowledge. In the meantime, she had work of her own to get on with.

One of the tabloids ran a piece on the Saturday

morning, another on the Sunday, complete with photographs. Between times the telephone hardly stopped ringing.

'Must be short on news,' commented Dave at one point. 'I thought only tennis stars merited this much interest!'

'You're a household name,' Sara reminded him. 'The public is entitled to know about your private life.'

His regard sharpened a little at her tone. 'No sense getting bitter about it. This is as far as it goes. Have you decided about the Australian tour, by the way? I'll need to be making arrangements.'

'I don't think I'll be coming,' she said on impulse. 'You're going to be pretty much tied up, and I've a couple of things I want to get on with.'

'Lost interest in the book we were supposed to be doing?' he asked on an odd note.

She avoided his eyes. 'I rather thought you had.'

'You could be right,' he agreed after a moment. 'It's already served its purpose.'

Getting her on that plane with him, for instance, came the thought. Only she doubted if marriage had been in his mind either at the time. They had both of them been carried away by the emotions of the moment—deluded into believing that wanting and loving were one and the same thing. Quite possibly she wasn't the only one who regretted that action. The difference being that Dave was apparently prepared to make the best of it, while she still hovered constantly in a state of flux. Perhaps a spell apart would be the best thing all round.

He left on a Thursday. At his own request, Sara didn't accompany him to the airport, where he would be meeting up with the rest of the team. Watching the car turn the corner of the road, she felt desolate, yet was also aware of a certain lifting of restriction. For two whole weeks she was free to do exactly as she pleased, eat when she felt like it, leave her tights drying over the shower rail without incurring Dave's masculine displeasure. He was tidy, if not fanatically so; she wasn't. He liked his meals at fairly regular intervals; she didn't. The only time they were really in accord was when making love, and they could hardly spend the whole of their time together doing that— although they certainly didn't practise very much restraint, she had to admit. All newly-weds must undergo the same period of adjustment to each other's habits, she realised. It was just that neither of them was ready to make any real effort in that direction.

Meeting Dave's mother again hadn't helped, but she had felt bound to make the gesture. It wouldn't last, Mrs Lyness had told her bluntly the moment she got her alone. She might have trapped Dave into marrying her but he'd soon come to his senses when he realised it was his money she was after. Sara had not attempted to reason with the woman. Proclaiming a deep and abiding love for her son was no answer when she couldn't be sure herself just how deep and how abiding it really was.

Mr Lyness had been a different matter. Best thing that ever happened to Dave, he had said when his wife was out of hearing. Apart from winning the championship, of course. He had named one of his best racer's offspring Sara in honour of the family addition. Sara had been both touched and amused. Not many had a pigeon as a namesake!

The first couple of days passed reasonably quickly. Maureen came in on the Saturday and insisted in whisking her off on a shopping expedition, finishing up with lunch at one of the big department stores in town.

'I hope you won't let anything my mother might say

get to you in any way,' she said frankly while they waited for their order. 'She'd have been the same whoever Dave married.'

'She can't really imagine I'm going to finish up spending all his winnings,' Sara responded with a smile. 'He's already offered to buy her a house of her own.'

'Ah, but what she'd really like is the money itself. Only Dave isn't stupid.'

'On the other hand, he can't expect anyone else to want the same things he wants.'

'Oh, I doubt if he does think that way. You can hardly blame him for not wanting to see it frittered away on rubbish.'

'I wasn't,' Sara said carefully, 'blaming him for anything. Whatever he does, it's his own affair.'

Maureen was looking at her with a curious expression. 'You don't feel you have any say in it yourself?'

'No. We're two people, not one.'

'Married couples can't afford to live separate lives. Not if they want to stay married.' The other laughed. 'I sometimes think that learning to share is the hardest part. James and I were on the verge of breaking up at least a couple of times.'

Blue eyes widened a fraction, intrigued by the notion. 'You were?'

'Oh, yes. He was a workaholic, you see. I hardly saw him after I left the firm when I was expecting the twins. There was even a time when I suspected him of having an affair with his new secretary. Anyway, we worked it out in the end.'

The message was obvious. Maureen wasn't stupid either, only the problem wasn't quite that simple. What the two of them had to work out was far more fundamental.

She drove herself out to Baslow on the Sunday at

Maureen's invitation, and spent a rainy afternoon helping entertain two hyper-active four-year-old boys.

'They're exhausting,' admitted their mother at seven when they were finally in bed. 'They haven't taken afternoon rests since they were babies. Roll on next year when they'll be in school!'

'You won't know what to do with yourself,' said James, pouring pre-dinner drinks. 'Just think of all that time to fill.'

'I'll manage,' returned his wife. 'I might even think about an Open University course. I never took any A-levels.'

'It's never too late.' James gave Sara her glass, glancing out at the rain still beading the window behind her. 'It isn't going to improve. Why don't you stay the night?'

'Yes, do,' urged Maureen. 'Dave often does.'

Smiling, Sara shook her head. 'It's nice of you to offer, but I've an article to get off first thing in the morning.'

'Work still coming your way then?' asked James, taking a seat.

'I had a couple of things in hand,' she acknowledged, 'but not everything I do is solicited.' She was looking into her glass as she spoke, gently swirling the contents. 'As a matter of fact, I'm thinking of taking a trip down to discuss one idea I've got with a certain magazine editor. It's an ideal time while Dave's away.'

'Yes, I suppose it is.' Maureen didn't sound too certain. 'Did you tell him when he phoned Friday?'

'No,' she said. 'I didn't decide until last night. But that's no problem. He won't be phoning again before Wednesday, and I'll be back by then.'

She wasn't being entirely honest, because the idea had only just crystallised in her mind. She felt buoyant, eager for a change of scene. Just a couple of days in familiar haunts, that was all she asked. She still had to do something about her flat down there anyway.

Only later, when she was driving back to town, did she finally break down and acknowledge what was really in her mind. Once she got away from here she wouldn't be coming back. Not on any permanent basis, at least. Dave had to be made to consider her viewpoint—her needs as well as his own. There were snooker clubs in the London area; his agent himself was based in Cheltenham, which was hardly that far out. They could keep on both flats, the way she had wanted to in the first place, and spend time between them. Not ideal, perhaps, but the marriage would stand more chance than it did right now. Whatever the outcome, she was through making all the sacrifices.

Arranging transportation of her repacked trunks at short notice, proved tricky. Tuesday afternoon was the earliest pick-up time available. It meant some rearrangement of plans, but nothing too drastic. She took it that Dave would probably ring Maureen when he received no reply on the Wednesday; he would guess the rest. As soon as he came back to England they could get together and discuss the situation like two rational adults.

The letter she left for him wasn't easy to compose. In the end she could only come up with a few terse lines. *I'm not ready to be a stay-at-home wife,* she wrote. *I'm not sure I ever could be. If you want to talk about it you know where to find me—only don't expect to persuade me the usual way because it won't work, Dave. We made one mistake, let's not compound it.*

Her trunks were picked up soon after lunch on the Tuesday, leaving her with just the two suitcases to handle herself. Loath to leave the Renault standing at the station, she booked a taxi to take her down for the four o'clock, and hoisted both bags downstairs one at a time in order to be ready to go the moment it came.

Opening the main door, she found Beryl Morton on the step, about to insert her key.

'One out, one in!' smiled the latter. 'We don't get to see much of each other.' Her eyes went beyond Sara to the two suitcases standing waiting in the hallway, her expression undergoing a sudden change. 'You're leaving?'

'I'm going back to London,' Sara agreed, thankful to see the taxi drawing up at the gate. 'You're not usually home at this time.'

'No, I snatched a couple of hours to do some shopping.' The hesitation was obvious. 'Anything I can do?' she asked lamely.

'I don't think so, thanks.' Sara hadn't allowed for any confrontations. The best she could manage was an apologetic shrug. 'Just one of those things. Glad to have met you, anyway.'

Beryl stayed in the doorway until the taxi drew away. She looked totally at a loss. Considering the circumstances, she had every reason, Sara conceded. She had come through the last two days without any feeling at all herself, apart from determination: how long that might last was anyone's guess. No matter what, she wasn't going to regret her action. It was the most sensible thing she had done in weeks.

CHAPTER NINE

WAKENING in that hotel bedroom, two years later, Sara lay for several minutes just gazing at the blank ceiling before stirring herself to get up. It had been around two before she had finally slept, and then only fitfully.

Going over it all again hadn't helped, she acknowledged. All she had succeeded in doing was opening old wounds. As the days had stretched into weeks and the weeks into months, with still no word from him, she had schooled herself into believing that things were better that way. Gradually, she had even managed to look on the whole affair with a certain amount of detachment. She still bore Dave's name but it had caused few problems.

It had taken Nigel to bring matters to a head; Nigel, who was everything any woman could possibly want in a husband. Resolve hardened again. She would leave no stone unturned when it came to gaining her freedom.

Dressed in the same grey suit she had worn the day before, though with a fresh white blouse, she checked out of the hotel a few minutes before eleven, carrying her overnight case outside to the front entrance where she could see the car arriving. The day wasn't fulfilling its early promise. There were dark clouds building over the Pennines, and a cool wind that made standing around uncomfortable. She wasn't sorry to see the silver-blue Jaguar coming up the drive.

'Sleep well? asked Dave casually when they were pulling away again.

'Fine, thanks.' She gave him a swift sideways glance, supremely conscious of his attraction in the suede jacket and roll-necked white sweater. 'Didn't you?'

'No,' he admitted. 'You brought back a whole lot of things I'd as soon not have remembered.'

'Perhaps I should have written after all.'

'It might have made things easier. Still, now that you are here we may as well take advantage of it. You can fill me in on the detail while we drive.'

'Such as what?' Sara queried, watching the passing houses.

'Such as why you want a divorce in such a hurry, for one thing.'

'So I can get married again,' she said, keeping her tone level. 'The man I'm to marry is going overseas in September. He wants to take me with him.'

The pause was lengthy, Dave's reaction difficult to assess. When he did speak he sounded quite calm about it. 'Who is he?'

'Sir Nigel Rotherby. He's a diplomat.'

'Wasn't he on the New Year Honours list?'

'That's right.' She was surprised he should be aware of it. 'The investiture was in February.'

'He must be twenty years older than you are.'

Her chin lifted a fraction. 'Almost twenty-three. So what? Youth doesn't hold a monopoly in marriage.'

'Like should marry like.'

'I agree,' she retorted smartly. 'Nigel and I have a lot in common.'

'So did we.'

'Only in one place. I got that out of my system a long time ago.'

His lips twisted. 'You mean he isn't all that highly sexed?'

'Oh, for God's sake!' Her voice held disgust. 'There's more to life than making it in bed!'

'You're right, there is. That might have been part of

our trouble. We never got round to trying it anywhere else.'

He was doing this deliberately, Sara reasoned, damping down the retort which sprang to her lips. It was just his way of getting at her. 'Our problems went rather deeper than that,' she said. 'Not that I'd expect you to understand what I'm talking about.'

'I understand fine. Money I can make, but I'd never have been able to offer you a title to go with it.'

Sara drew in a shaky breath. 'You think that's all I'm interested in?'

The shrug held derision. 'So tell me you're crazy about him. Tell me you'd marry him if even if he'd started life as a cockney barrow-boy!'

'As a matter of fact, yes, I would. It's what a man makes of himself that counts, not what he's born.'

'There was a time when I might have believed you really meant that. I learned the hard way.'

She swallowed, suddenly and painfully. 'I doubt if it went that deep, or you'd have made some effort to contact me.'

'I didn't say it went deep. Anyway. there wasn't much point. That note of yours said it all.'

He put his foot down as they turned out of the main stream of traffic, sending the car zooming forward with scant attention to any speed restrictions. Sara stole a glance at the hard profile and felt the iron band about her chest constrict a little more. If he said no to what she was asking of him she was sunk. It was going to be another year before she could even apply for a divorce under English law, and perhaps as much as six months after that before a decree became absolute. Nigel would wait for her, of course, but they wouldn't be together. He could hardly afford to take another man's wife with him to the Embassy.

Her approach could have been a little more diplomatic, she was bound to concede. Male pride being what it was, Dave wasn't going to make this easy for her. She would have to begin again, with more care this time.

She said tentatively, 'I'm sorry if we got off on the wrong foot. I didn't mean it to be like this.'

'A civilised chat, was that the idea?'

'It wasn't a bad one.'

'Except that I don't feel particularly civilised about any of it.' He paused before adding brusquely, 'Look, let's just leave it for a while, shall we? Give me an hour or so to think about it.'

He had had all night, she wanted to point out, but refrained. By hook or by crook she would drag an answer from him before she returned home!

They went to another of the Derbyshire village pubs for a lunch of grilled rainbow trout with almondine sauce, following it up with a lemon mousse so light it melted in the mouth. Dave was recognised from all sides, the congratulations flowing thick and fast.

'The difference two years can make,' he commented at one point. 'The last time we did this I was a comparative newcomer to the pro game, this time my face is better known.'

'It's been getting some coverage,' she agreed. 'You won just about everything worth winning this last season, to say nothing of the TV and magazine advertising. I read about the boys' club opening, by the way. Is it a success?'

'They're coming in. That's a start. I'm planning on opening another in Leeds this back end.' The pause held a certain deliberation. 'I don't have anything else much to spend my earnings on.'

'What about your family?' she asked, ignoring the innuendo.

He shrugged. 'Still in the same place. Jimmy's at the local comprehensive now.'

'Doing well?'

'Not so as you'd notice. He's formed a group. It's all he talks about these days. Buying him a guitar was the worse thing I ever did.'

'Are they any good?'

'Does it matter? They don't stand a chance in hell of getting anywhere.'

Sara wasn't going to argue that point. 'How are Maureen and James?' she asked instead.

'Very little change there either. You wouldn't expect it, would you?'

She sighed. 'Dave, I'm trying to make this easy for both of us. You're not helping.'

'I already told you, I don't think much to these civilised arrangements.'

'So what's the alternative?'

The green eyes were slightly narrowed, expression suddenly calculating. 'I'll want something in return.'

Sara's heart came up into her throat. She swallowed, unable to look away. 'Such as?'

'Help with a problem of my own. Her name is Ann.'

The sudden heaviness in the pit of her stomach needed no analysis. Don't be dog-in-the-manger about this, Sara told herself, fighting the reaction. Dave had as much right as she did to seek solace elsewhere.

'So what's the problem?' she managed with creditable steadiness.

His shoulders lifted briefly. 'She's starting to take over my life.'

'If you're finding it difficult to ditch her you must have given her the impression there was more in it than you obviously feel.'

A spark lit his eyes. 'Are you asking me or telling me?'

'Suggesting,' she came back. 'Why not try the blunt approach?'

'I was getting round to it before you turned up.'

Blue eyes darkened. 'You're not using me as an excuse!'

'I can't think of a better. She'd hardly stand in the way of a reconciliation between man and wife.'

'Except that it isn't going to be, is it?'

'She doesn't have to know that.'

Sara forced herself to look him squarely in the face. 'Just what is it you had in mind?'

'Let her find you there at the flat tonight. She's coming round to make me a home-cooked meal.'

'Her idea or yours?'

'Hers.' His tone mocked. 'The way to a man's heart, don't you know?'

Not this man's, she thought. He didn't have one. Aloud, she said, 'I have to be back in London tonight. In any case, you don't need my actual presence.'

'Let's say I'd prefer it.'

Beneath the cover of the table, her nails bit into her palms. 'If you think you're going to get anything out of this . . .'

'Not just me,' he said, 'both of us. You want my co-operation, don't you?'

Sara wasn't sure what she wanted—or felt either, for that matter. Reluctance, certainly, but it went further than that. She supposed fear was the only word that fitted the emotion: fear of what else might be going on behind those cynical green eyes. Dave was capable of using her in more ways than the one.

'If I do it,' she said at length, 'I'm not staying any longer than need be. Once your girlfriend is out of the way, I follow. She's hardly likely to come back.'

'Depends how far you go towards convincing her it wouldn't be any use. She's tenacious.'

'Or besotted.' Her throat hurt. She remembered only too well what that feeling was like. 'You're a bastard, Dave!'

'Probably. I'm not too hot when it comes to picking the right woman, for sure. Maybe I should settle for the one-night stands.'

'They're more your weight,' she agreed caustically, 'variety being the spice of life, and all that! I'll need to make a phone call.'

'You can do that from the flat.'

There was little else to be said. He had her in a cleft stick. Sara closed her mind to the images memory kept dredging up from the depths. Nothing was going to happen between them. She'd make sure of that. A few hours weren't going to make any difference to anything.

Shorn of the need to get her to the station, Dave showed no inclination to hurry the rest of the meal. With conversation impersonal, Sara even found herself beginning to relax a little. There was no real reason, she supposed, to suspect his motives. He just wanted out of an awkward situation. Even if this Ann subsequently discovered that the supposed reconciliation had not been a success, the break would have been made. The thought of him with another woman still got to her, she had to admit. Obviously they were on intimate terms. The bedroom they themselves had once shared would no doubt have known many visitors since her departure, and would probably know others after this. Only next time he got himself embroiled he would have to extricate himself, because she wasn't going to be around.

It was well past three by the time they reached the flat.

'Use the extension in the bedroom,' Dave invited with a certain irony when Sara made a move towards the telephone. 'More private.'

'It doesn't matter,' she said coolly. 'I shan't be saying anything you can't listen in to.'

She dialled the number, spoke briefly with the secretary who answered, and heard the familiar, well-bred voice on the other end of the line with a sense of reassurance. 'Nigel, I'm afraid I'm going to be late,' she said without beating about the bush. 'I'm not sure what time.'

'Having problems?' he asked.

'Nothing that can't be handled.' She had her head turned away from the man lounging on the sofa, but she could almost sense the sardonic lift of an eyebrow. 'I'll phone you in the morning. Sorry about dinner.'

'It will keep,' he said. 'Thank you for letting me know, Sara. I'll wait for your call.'

No tender farewells, no fond endearments, she reflected wryly, putting down the receiver. But there wouldn't be, of course, not on an open line. Nigel reserved such expressions of his feelings for times when they were securely alone.

'No questions, no complaints?' asked Dave as she turned, echoing the pattern if not the content of her thoughts. 'The man must trust you.'

'He does,' she said succinctly, not about to admit that he knew nothing of her real whereabouts. 'The same way I trust him.'

He eyed her in silence for a moment, jawline hard. 'How long have you known him?'

'Since January. I did a profile on him for *World* magazine.'

'I saw it. I said *known*.'

Of all the people, Dave was still the one who could bring her closest to losing all sense of proportion, Sara acknowledged, struggling to retain it. She said tautly, 'You've no damned right to ask, much less get an answer, but I'll give you one anyway. I haven't slept with him. Not yet.'

His expression didn't alter as far as she could see. 'Because you haven't wanted it, or because he doesn't?'

'Because we happen to have a relationship based on more important issues!'

'You're kidding yourself.' His head was still back against the cushion, but the line of his body was tense. 'I've had you, sweetheart. I know what you need from a man.'

'From you, perhaps, because that's all you were capable of giving.' Her eyes were bright, blazing blue. 'Even then it didn't take long to pall! There hasn't been a moment in these past two years when I've missed any part of you, Dave!'

The tension in the room was almost visual, stretched like a wire between them. He was getting purposefully to his feet when the doorbell rang, stopping him in his tracks.

'She's early,' he said. 'I wasn't expecting her before six.'

Sara drew in a long breath, limbs nerveless as she groped for the chair-arm behind her and supported her weight. 'Don't you think you'd better let her in before she takes it you're not here?' she suggested with a valiant attempt to sound cool and in control. 'Early or late, it's what I'm here for, isn't it?'

Face set, he got up and went out to the lobby. Sara heard the door open, and a light female voice, 'The main door was open so I came right on up. They put the Leeds demo back till Thursday so I've got an extra couple of hours. How does liver and onions with new potatoes and peas sound to a hungry man?' There was a pause, a sudden change of tone. 'Is something wrong?'

'There's someone here you'd better meet,' said Dave. 'In the living-room.'

Sara steeled herself as a pair of them came through the inner door. Ann was slim and blonde and attractive—no less than she might have anticipated. About her own age, or even a year or so older, she assessed. Her expression was guarded.

'My wife,' said Dave. 'Ann Paramore, Sara.'

The other was the first to speak. 'I seem to have chosen a bad time to visit.'

'It's a classic situation,' Sara agreed coolly, 'but I'm sure we can all be adult about it, can't we?'

Ann was quite obviously at a loss for an answer to that question. Her gaze shifted to the man now standing a few feet away, appealing for help. 'You should have phoned me.'

'You'd said you were going to be in Leeds all day,' he responded, giving little away. 'I'm sorry, Ann.'

Colour came and went in her face, leaving her looking suddenly drained. Sara stifled the impulse to add her own apologies. It was out of character for the wife to feel sympathy with the mistress. 'What he's trying to say is we've decided to try again,' she said. 'It's what we both want.'

'Just like that, after two years?' The other girl's voice was shaky.

Sara kept her own voice level. 'I've been here since last night.'

The colour came again. 'Oh,' she said. 'I see.'

'I'm sure you do.' She couldn't take much more of this, Sara told herself. 'I think it might be a good idea if you just left,' she forced out. 'It would save a lot of awkwardness.'

Ann's eyes were on Dave, wide and dark, 'Why didn't you tell me before?'

'Because I didn't know,' he said.

'You must have had some idea!'

'No, he didn't.' She was already into this, Sara acknowledged ruefully; she might as well make a proper job of it. 'I wasn't sure myself until I got here. Not that it makes any difference, anyway. I'm here, that's the main point.'

'Until you walk out on him again?'

'It remains to be seen. Whether we stay together or not isn't really your concern, is it?'

'Put like that, I don't suppose it is.' Ann was still looking at Dave, face stiff. 'You never really cared about me, did you? I was just a stand-in.' She didn't wait for any answer. 'I'll go, don't worry. There's nothing to stay for. I hope you'll both be very happy!'

He went with her to the door. Sara listened to the murmur of voices, heard the outer door close and stiffened herself as Dave came back into the room. 'Louse,' she exclaimed bitterly. 'Do you give a damn about anyone or anything outside of your own interests?'

He moved abruptly, going over to the drinks cupboard to take out bottle and glass and pour himself a stiff measure. 'She'll get over it. You're a resilient sex.'

'We have to be when there are men like you around. How much did you tell her about us?'

'Just the bare details.'

'With all the blame laid at my door, of course.'

'As a matter of fact, no. A fair share of it was mine.'

She stared at him, momentarily disconcerted. 'That's quite an admission, coming from you. Where do you think you went wrong?'

'Not coming after you with a damn' big stick!'

Her breath came out on a faint sigh. 'I should have known! You haven't learned a thing these last two years.'

He turned to look at her, outwardly unmoved by the statement. 'You think you have?'

'Enough.' Her knuckles were white where they gripped the chair back. 'I discovered the difference between sexual attraction and real emotion, for one thing.'

'From your lover?'

'He isn't my lover,' she said between her teeth. 'I already told you that.'

'I'll have to fill him in on what gets you going.'

'He wouldn't be interested in your swashbuckling techniques!'

The laugh was harsh. 'But you are.'

'Not since I grew up. These days I prefer a little finesse—a quality you wouldn't know much about.' The words came out like barbed darts, each one precisely aimed. 'You'd have been in your element tumbling milkmaids in the hay, Dave. They wouldn't have known the difference either!'

The sudden glint in the green eyes was unnerving. He reached behind him to put down the glass without taking his attention from her face. 'We might be short on the hay,' he said, 'but the tumble can be arranged.'

She made no move as he came over to her. Even when he took her roughly by the arms and dragged her up to him she refused to struggle. Instead she kept her lips tight and closed, her body quite still, her eyes wide open. Nothing he could do was going to reach her. Not in any way!

Except she was wrong about that too, because it was already happening, her limbs trembling, heat flaring, her mouth beginning to soften, to allow him entry. With the chair at her back there was no way of escape. He had her pinned against the wing, his hand already thrusting its way inside the silk blouse, the touch of his fingers on her breast awakening memories so powerful she could scarcely contain the swift surge of emotion. In that one searing moment she wanted everything he had ever done to her.

It was Dave himself who did the drawing back. He was breathing harshly, but he was still in control.

'That's one way you haven't changed,' he said. 'I hope this Nigel of yours can take you the same distance.'

Sara took a grip on herself, drawing the front edges of her blouse together with fingers that felt numb. 'You mean you hope he can't! You'd love to believe you were the only man in the world with that kind of acumen, wouldn't you, Dave?'

'Don't try telling me it isn't important to you again,' he came back, ignoring the jibe. 'You just proved differently. I could have taken you all the way without any problem.'

'So why didn't you?' she challenged, trying not to let the tremor show up in her voice. 'If you're so damned confident, why stop there?'

His mouth twisted. 'Because there's no way you're going to goad me into giving you what you're after.'

'What I'm after?'

'The real reason you're here—to get yourself laid.' He blocked the vicious swing of her hand with a swiftly raised forearm. 'Don't let's start a rough-house. I'm no gentleman, remember?'

'As if I needed any reminder!' Biting her lip, Sara nursed the wrist she had smashed into his. 'I was right earlier. You really are a bastard!'

'If I am you made me one. You turn up out of the blue after two years with some crazy excuse and start right in needling me—how else am I supposed to react?'

'There's nothing crazy about wanting a divorce!'

'So why not consult a lawyer?'

'There isn't much point if it turns out to be no go anyway from the American end. It's another year before we can apply here.'

'So you keep telling me.'

'It's true.' She was doing her best to restrain her temper. 'I came here with a simple enough request. Reno is almost next door to Tahoe. All you have to do is get a few details. If it's necessary for one of us to establish residence for a time, I'll take care of that. You won't need to do anything else except sign the papers. I shan't be asking for a settlement, if that's what you're afraid of!'

He was standing back, away from her, hands thrust into trouser pockets, eyes steely. 'That crack's going to cost you.'

She said thickly, 'Refusing isn't going to change anything in the long run.'

'I didn't say I was going to refuse.'

The pause stretched. Sara wished she could sort out the utter confusion in her mind. 'So what did you have in mind?' she made herself ask.

'That's simple enough too, only it isn't a request. Like you said last night, it took two of us to get into this, it's going to take two of us to get out of it. If you want to know the chances of a fast divorce you come right along with me.'

He was moving away as he spoke, going across to take up the glass he had discarded and drain the contents before turning back to look at her. 'Nothing to say?'

'Is anything I could say going to make any difference?' Her voice sounded rough.

'No.'

'Then I'm not going to waste any breath. If I do go to Nevada I'll be travelling separately and staying separately.'

'You'll be going my way, or not at all.'

A pulse jerked suddenly at her temple. 'What am I supposed to deduce from that?'

'Whatever you damn' well like. Just be at Heathrow a week on Sunday with a valid passport.' He glanced at the empty glass still in his hand as if contemplating a refill, then shrugged and put it down. 'Tidy yourself up and I'll take you down for the five-twenty.' His brows lifted at her change of expression. 'That's what you want, isn't it?'

'Of course,' she said swiftly. 'The sooner the better.'

'Then get moving. It's nearly five now.'

There was to be no further discussion on the

subject; his attitude made that all too painfully clear. The decision was to be entirely hers. She had, Sara realised, less than two weeks in which to make it.

CHAPTER TEN

THEY were at the station by ten minutes past the hour. Dave didn't offer to accompany her on to the platform.

'Phone me when you've made up your mind,' he said. 'Only don't leave it too long or I might change mine.'

Searching the unrelenting features, Sara knew what impotence really meant. It took every ounce of willpower she had to turn and walk away from him without attempting one more appeal to his better nature. It wouldn't be any use. He was relishing the whole situation.

The train was almost empty. She took a window seat, resting her head back against the cover and closing her eyes as the whistle sounded and doors banged. The last time she had made this journey she had been running away. If she had given it more time, put a little more effort into making Dave understand how she felt, they might still have been together. The problems which two years ago had seemed so insurmountable could have been sorted out in the end.

Too late now, of course. The attraction might still exist but the softer emotions were dead. What he really wanted was revenge, hence the ultimatum. What worried her was how far that desire might go. This afternoon had proved her own weakness when it came to resistance. He could still undermine every moral fibre she possessed. Feeling the way she did about Nigel was no defence against her baser instincts. One determined assault on Dave's part and she would be lost. If she went with him to Nevada she would have to watch every step, every word: no provocation of any kind. He would leave her alone if she left him alone. At least she could hope he would.

She was in London by eight, and home by eight-thirty. The flat felt cold and lonely. It wasn't too late to telephone Nigel, but she didn't feel like facing that particular problem tonight. By tomorrow she had to be able to look him in the eye and pretend everything was going to be plain sailing. He might be angry that she had taken it on herself to go this far without prior discussion, but he would surely appreciate her motives. Once they were married she would devote herself to being the kind of wife he needed; one he could be proud of. It would be her lifetime's work.

She spent the evening working on a survey commissioned by one of the diet magazines, finishing around eleven with a sigh of relief. The bread-and-butter work paid for self-indulgence in other directions, but it lacked stimulation. When it all boiled down, the only sure way of keeping down weight was to practise self-control. So far it wasn't one of her problems, thank heaven. There could be nothing more boring than being constantly aware of every calorie.

The intercom buzzer went while she was in the kitchen making herself a bedtime drink. Nigel sounded apologetic over the line.

'I was passing close so thought I'd take a chance on your being back,' he said. 'May I come up?'

'Of course.' There was little else, Sara reflected wryly, that she could say. She pressed the door release, taking a swift glance in the mirror above it as she did so. She looked tired, the smudge of carbon on her cheek matching the dark circles under her eyes. Too late to do much about it, except remove the smudge. She went back to the kitchen to find a damp cloth, returning in time to open the door on the first soft knock.

Sir Nigel Rotherby was not a big man in stature. He topped Sara by only an inch or two, but his lack of height did nothing to detract from his appearance in her eyes. The dark hair brushed with silver at the temples and calm, intelligent features never failed to rouse warmth in her heart. Distinguished was the word she would have applied if asked to describe his looks. It was the one which had sprung to mind the moment they had met. She responded to his kiss with honest affection.

'Have you been out all evening?' she asked as they went through to the sitting-room. 'I was going to phone earlier, but I decided to leave it until morning.'

'I went to the club,' he said. 'To be truthful, I wasn't sure you'd be back at all tonight.'

Sara felt her stomach muscles contract. She made herself meet his eyes. 'What made you think that?'

His regard was steady. 'Something in your voice when you spoke to me this afternoon. You didn't sound yourself.' He paused, waiting, adding when she failed to speak, 'Aren't you going to tell me about it?'

'There isn't a lot to tell,' she said. 'Why don't you sit down and I'll get you a drink.'

'I'll pass up the drink. I'm using the car.' He studied her for a moment, then reached out and took her hand, drawing her down to a seat on the sofa behind them. 'All right, so now we're both sitting comfortably. Shall we begin?'

She laughed, appreciating the gentle humour. 'It's obvious which programmes you watch!'

'There's a lot to be said for the simpler things in life,' he returned equably. 'And you're evading the question.'

'Not really.' She let her hand rest where it was in his palm. 'I went to see Dave.'

He was silent for a moment, searching her face with sudden intensity. Characteristically, he made no reference to her bending of the truth. What couldn't be altered had to be endured was one of the maxims he lived by. 'With what purpose? The way the law stands . . .'

'I told him I wanted to try for an American divorce,' she said. 'He's going to Nevada in a couple of weeks. I thought he stood a better chance of finding out what the chances are on the spot.'

Nigel shook his head. 'My dear, the chances may be excellent, but it doesn't necessarily mean it would be valid over here. I take it you haven't consulted a lawyer?'

'Not yet,' she admitted, 'I didn't see any reason. Whatever the odds, I'm willing to take them. An American wedding, an American divorce. If the one is legal, I don't see why the other shouldn't be.'

'It's a debatable point.' He hesitated before voicing the question. 'I gather he wasn't very co-operative?'

'Only insofar as he isn't going to have time to go into it himself.'

'Ah!' The exclamation was soft. 'You mean he wants you to go with him.'

She said quickly, 'I suppose it makes sense when you think about it. With luck, we can get the whole thing sorted out in a few days. If it turned out to be necessary to establish residence for a time, I could stay on.'

Nigel was looking at her oddly. 'You seem to have given the matter a lot of thought.'

'I have. Only I didn't want to mention it as a possibility in case Dave turned awkward.'

'He obviously needed a lot of persuasion if it took you two whole days to get him to agree.'

'Hardly that much,' she protested. 'I didn't get to see him at all until fairly late last night, so we agreed to leave it till this morning. I spent the night in a hotel, of course.'

Nigel smiled a little. 'I don't doubt that.'

'Meaning you do doubt the rest?'

'I just don't see it being that simple. Oh, the American end, perhaps. I mean here.'

'It's a chance worth taking, isn't it? You know the alternative.' She paused there, tone altering. 'Unless you've changed your mind about me?'

'I haven't changed my mind.' The words were quietly spoken but none the less sincere. 'I'm not sure that you shouldn't change yours. I waited a long time for the right woman to come along, Sara, but I have to admit I never anticipated she'd be so many years my junior. Have you really thought about what it will be like when I'm in my seventies and you're still a relatively young woman—provided we even lasted that long?'

'We agreed to forget about the age thing,' she reminded him. 'It makes no difference.' She leaned forward and kissed him, finding comfort in his restrained embrace. His kisses might not do as much for her as Dave's did, but they didn't leave her cold either. As a lover he would be gentle, tender—all the things Dave wasn't. He wanted her, she knew that. It was just that she needed everything to be right first.

He left before midnight, resigned to her decision to make the trip, if not very happy about it. Going back over everything he had said as she prepared for bed, Sara wondered if he had spoken the whole truth. That his feelings for her were genuine she couldn't doubt, but weighing everything in balance he could well decide that the difficulties were going to be too many. From the first the relationship had been kept under wraps. In his position, he couldn't afford the wrong kind of publicity. She wasn't sure what her own reactions might be if he did change his mind about marrying her. The only thing she was sure of was that she was going ahead with plans already made. Whatever happened, she still wanted her freedom.

Interest in the new world snooker champion had already been usurped by other sporting events, in the nationals at least. The call from Jeff Brady that following morning took her completely by surprise.

'Are you and Dave planning on getting it together again?' he queried without preamble.

'What makes you think we might be?' Sara asked cautiously.

'A colleague saw you up there on Monday. Just happened to mention it in passing.'

'Only to you?'

'So far as I know. Made me wonder, that's all.'

'Well, you can forget it.'

'Okay, don't get shirty.' The pause was brief, his tone over-casual. 'Heard another snippet I thought you should know about.'

Sara felt the pulse throb suddenly at her temple. 'Such as?'

'Concerns that guy you did the profile on—Rotherby. Seems he's got himself involved with some kid half his age. Not what you'd expect from a man in his position.'

And they had been so careful, she thought. The only other person who knew about it besides the two of them was Nigel's secretary, and she was far too circumspect to allow a word to pass her lips. She had told Dave, of course, but he was hardly likely to have released the information. In any case, there would hardly have been time. Aloud she said, 'Why tell me?'

'Oh, come on!' Jeff's tone was derisive. 'If I can put two and two together, so can others. The connection's there.'

'Hardly conclusive.'

'It only takes a whisper to start an avalanche, you know that. The age difference he might get away with at a pinch, the fact that his lady-love already has a husband who isn't exactly an unknown is something else. If he's too far in to see it for himself, I'm surprised you'd let him take that kind of risk, Sara.'

'It isn't the way you might think.' Her throat felt tight. 'Jeff, this is just between the two of us, and I'm trusting you. We're going to be married as soon as I can get a divorce.'

There was a small silence before he spoke again. 'Dave's in agreement, then?'

'Yes.' It was almost a relief to talk about it. 'Nigel's posting makes it essential I get it through fast, and Reno's the only place for that. I'm going out there the same time as Dave so we can get things moving right away.' She added urgently, 'You will keep it to yourself, won't you, Jeff?'

'Sure, it's hardly in my line. Thought I should offer a friendly warning, that's all.'

'And I'm grateful for it. We'll take more care in future.'

'Just hope you know what you're doing this time,' he tagged on heavily before ringing off.

It was some time before Sara could stir herself to any kind of action. The very least she could do was tell Nigel what Jeff had told her, she decided in the end. They might even have to stop seeing each other for a while. The last thing she would want was to harm his career.

He wasn't available when she rang. She left a message with his secretary, for the first time wondering if the woman's quiet, rather dowdy exterior accurately reflected her hidden emotions. She had been with her employer several years, and secretaries were renowned for falling in love with their bosses. It could even be she who had begun the rumour Jeff had heard. Unlikely, she had to admit. Even if the woman did harbour a secret passion, she was hardly going to risk hurting the source of it in any way.

Sara was out herself all afternoon, arriving home

around six. Showered, and clad in a bathrobe, she began preparing the ingredients for a light supper. Nigel wouldn't be here before nine, and he never ate a lot in the evenings anyway. With the salad in the refrigerator, and the quiche she had made earlier all ready to reheat in the oven, she laid the table and opened the Beaujolais to allow it time to breathe. All that remained now was to get dressed.

She was on her way to the bedroom when the buzzer went. A glance at her watch told her it was unlikely to be Nigel yet: probably someone pressing the wrong button, she thought, going to answer it. It often happened. Dave's voice came as a shock in more ways than the one. He had been in and out of her mind all day.

'I want to sée you,' he said.

'You could have phoned,' she protested.

'The way you did me?'

He had a point. Biting her lips, she released the door. It was only just after eight, but that was little comfort. It all depended on what he was here to say.

Only when she went to let him in did she realise she was still wearing the bathrobe. Dave eyed her long, bare legs with a lift of his brows.

'Expecting someone else?'

'I've been in the shower,' she responded stiffly. 'What are you doing in London?'

'Chat show,' he said succinctly. 'You obviously didn't see it.'

'I haven't had the set on since I came in.'

'Pity. Your name came into it.'

Her breath caught. '*My* name?'

'That's what I said.' They had moved on into the sitting-room. His glance rested briefly on the ready-laid table. 'Cosy. What time are you expecting him?'

'Not for another hour or so.' She stuck her hands

deep in her pockets, wishing she didn't feel quite so much at a disadvantage. 'Why?'

If he had said why what, she would have thrown something at him, but he didn't. 'Local newspaper report sparked it off, I imagine.' He slanted a glance. 'You knew about that?'

'No.' Her heart had missed a beat. 'When?'

'This morning. They ran quite a piece. Reliable sources have it we're definitely on again.'

Her brows drew together. 'No one else . . .' She stopped there, eyes darkening. 'Your girlfriend?'

'She'd be the obvious one to supply confirmation.'

'So your affair was public knowledge?'

'We didn't try hiding it, if that's what you mean.' Dave was watching her with an enigmatic expression. 'Is it that important?'

'It is to me. You denied it, of course?'

'Not in so many words. I let it be known I considered it nobody else's business but our own.'

'That's as good as an admission!'

'Not to me.' He sounded unmoved. 'I wouldn't say no to a drink if it were offered.'

'You know where they are,' she came back shortly. 'Help yourself.'

He moved to comply. 'How about you?'

About to say no, she abruptly changed her mind. 'I'll have vodka. On the rocks.'

Bringing both glasses back to where she had sunk to a seat on the sofa, he passed hers to her before sitting down himself in the chair opposite. 'How long have you been hitting the hard stuff?'

'Since now,' she said. 'I need some extra backbone.' She took a drink from the glass, grimaced, and put it down again. 'Maybe not that badly.' There was a lengthy pause. She didn't look at him as she said unsteadily, 'I'd like you to finish your drink and go, Dave. As soon as possible.'

'Before your visitor arrives?'

'If you put it like that, yes.'

'I'd like to meet him,' he stated. 'I think I'm entitled to that, at least.'

Sara was tense, trying not to push. 'What point is there.'

His smile was faint. 'You were the one who wanted a civilised arrangement. What could be better than the three people involved sitting down to thrash out the detail together?'

'There's nothing else to talk about.'

'So call it curiosity.'

'You're trying to ruin things for me, aren't you?' she accused. 'I wouldn't put it past you to have engineered that press report yourself!' She got to her feet, shaky but resolved. 'I'm going to get dressed. If you've a shred of decency left, you'll be gone by the time I'm ready.'

With the bedroom door closed at her back, she stood for a moment to gather herself. What she would do if Dave was still there when she emerged again she wasn't at all certain. The least she could do was telephone Nigel now on the bedroom extension and warn him—leave it to him to decide whether he wanted to face the situation. The other thing would have to wait.

She was sitting on the edge of the bed in the act of dialling the number when Dave came into the room. He had taken off his jacket and tie. As she stared at him frozenly, he began to unbutton his shirt.

'Put that down,' he said.

Asking him what he thought he was doing would be a totally superfluous question, she thought numbly. 'I want you out of here,' she forced through stiff lips. '*Now!*'

'Not yet,' he said. 'Not until we've settled at least one question.'

'No!' She was standing, but there was nowhere to go. He was between her and the door. Her voice trembled suddenly. 'Dave, don't!'

He continued to remove his clothing, movements unhurried. 'I want you, Sara. And you still want me. I can feel it from here.'

Seeing him naked brought a rush of blood to her head; she could hear it drumming in her ears. She made some futile little gesture of protest as he came to her, brushed aside with assertion. The belt of her robe came open to his pull, affording him freedom to slide both hands in and around her body.

The contact made her shiver, not with dread but with swift and sudden arousal. Her lips parted to his, tongues touching, tasting, senses flaming. She felt his male hardness pressuring her thighs, the urgency in his loins, the wonderful wild hunger sweeping though her.

If there had ever been any real desire to escape it was gone now. She wanted to be closer, a part of him; to have him inside her, filling her. Nothing had changed; nothing ever would change. They were a matched pair. How could she deny it?

He slid the robe from her arms before laying her down on the bed, his mouth scorching as it moved from throat to breast, his tongue a torment in its erotic exploration of each rosy-peaked nipple, fluttering her stomach muscles in its slow and subtle progression, drawing her breath when he parted her thighs. It was too much, much too much; she couldn't bear it! Her lips formed his name, over and over, pleading with him, begging him, the sounds running together until they were no longer coherent. Then he was moving back on top of her, sliding slowly inside her, hands lifting her hips to his long, deep thrusts; urging her to wilder and wilder response until he could himself no longer hold out against the greater need. Like

Catherine wheels, she thought mistily as the earth tilted on its axis.

Even when she could think again, she could find neither sorrow nor shame for what had happened. For the first time in two long years, her body felt at rest. Satisfaction was the word, she supposed. One might achieve a certain physical appeasement alone, but nothing could replace the real thing. Only not just any man. Not for her, anyway. Dave could reach the innermost part of her—sense what she needed before she knew it herself. She had missed his lovemaking so much. How much she was only just beginning to acknowledge.

He was still lying on top of her, his face buried in the crook of her shoulder. Sara thought he might have fallen asleep. She held her breath when he stirred, willing him to stay where he was until she had her emotions in some kind of order. If only they could just stay here like this for ever. Bed held no problems. It was the world outside that created those.

When he rolled over on to his back she felt chilled, although the room was warm enough.

'I needed that,' he said. 'So did you. You'd find it difficult to do without, Sara.'

Her voice sounded hollow. 'You think a man of forty-eight is going to be past providing it?'

'Keeping pace might be the problem. Something has to go. He isn't going to get any younger, and that's a fact.'

'Neither am I.'

'You know what I'm talking about. The gap won't narrow, it only gets wider.'

'With compensations.' She sat up suddenly, swinging her feet to the floor. 'You wouldn't understand about that. To you, sex is everything!'

'Not everything, just a good proportion.' His hands came about her hips, his lips finding the hollow at the base of her spine. 'Again,' he murmured against her skin. 'I want you again, Sara.'

'No!' She tore herself away from him, limbs shaky as she scooped up the bathrobe from the floor. 'Go away, Dave. Please go away!'

'So you can pretend it never happened?' He was sitting up himself now, lip curled. 'Not as easy as that, sweetheart.'

Sara tied the belt tightly about her waist, forcing herself to turn and look him squarely in the eye. 'You're planning on throwing it in Nigel's face?'

'Maybe I will, maybe I won't. You'll just have to wait and see, won't you?'

She said bitterly, 'You really are a bastard!'

'So you keep telling me.' The smile was dangerous. 'And I'm going to keep right on being one.'

If there had been any point in trying to make him see reason, there wasn't going to be time, she realised. Unless they got a move on, Nigel would be arriving before either of them was dressed. It would be of little consequence anyway if Dave intended telling all, but she couldn't be sure of that. He would probably extract a great deal of amusement out of watching her squirm. Confession would be even harder. Nigel might forgive her; he certainly couldn't be expected to understand. In any case that would have to come later if it came at all. Right now it would be enough to get through the evening.

Dave watched her gather her clothing together, without moving from the bed. She took them into the bathroom, closing and locking the door in her wake. Too late, of course. She should have done that earlier. Except that she didn't have a lock on her bedroom. There had never seemed any need until now. The face reflected in the mirror looked flushed, eyes dark and secretive. Her body still retained the imprint of his hands, still tingled from his caresses; still yearned. Why couldn't he have just left her alone?

He was dressed again and back in the sitting-room when she emerged. Her choice of slim grey skirt and toning silk blouse met with sardonic approval.

'Classy,' he said, 'just right for a lady. What time are you expecting him?'

'Any minute.' She added stonily, 'I'm going to have trouble stretching the meal to three.'

'You can always make out you're on a diet,' he retorted. 'Try laying another place for starters.'

Sara went to comply, conscious of his eyes following her across the room. He had proved his power: he didn't care about her feelings. But then he never had.

She was almost convinced Nigel wasn't going to make it after all when the quarter came and went without a sign. It was twenty-five minutes past the hour before the buzzer sounded, by which time her nerves were already in shreds. Dave stayed right where he was on the sofa when she went to open the door.

Nigel was full of apologies. He'd been tied up until nine, and unable to telephone, he said. Sara had been rehearsing in her mind what she was going to say, but all she managed when it came right down to it was the bald announcement.

'Dave's here.'

The disconcertment was swiftly overcome. 'Hadn't you better introduce us?' he suggested equably.

The younger man got to his feet as the two of them entered the room. Sara performed the superfluous ceremony, thankful that neither of the two offered to shake hands.

'Dave was on tonight's chat show,' she added into the resultant pause. 'I don't suppose you saw it, Nigel?'

'No,' he admitted, 'I mostly just watch the news items. Congratulations on your win, by the way.'

'Thanks.' Dave was sitting down again, one leg

propped comfortably across the other. 'I had a run of luck.'

'Rather more than that, I think. You have to know your game.'

'You've played yourself?'

'I play billiards. The skills required are much the same.'

The faint smile spoke volumes. 'I'm sure. Sorry to butt in like this, there were a few details I needed to get straight.'

'I must see to the supper,' said Sara hastily. 'It's going to be burned to a crisp!'

She could hear the murmur of voices while she was in the kitchen, neither of them raised. Guilt was a knife stabbing her in the chest. She couldn't get through a couple of hours of this, she thought desperately. She just couldn't! Dave was going to make her sweat, there was nothing surer. It was right there in his eyes when she looked at him. She deserved it, she supposed. She'd hardly fought very hard to reject him a while back. In some respects it would be almost a relief if he did carry out the implied threat. Anything was better than feeling the way she did at the moment.

There was no hint when she took in the soup of what might have transpired in her absence. Both men were past masters of the closed expression. It was about the only characteristic they did share. Seated between the two of them at the table, Sara attempted to make some kind of conversation, aware she was talking too fast and too loud but unable to stand the pauses either.

'It was Dave himself who put a stop to it in the end. 'Don't try so hard,' he advised bluntly. 'You're not improving anything.'

'You caused the situation in the first place,' she reminded him in swift anger. 'I'm simply trying to make the best of it!'

'I think it might be best if we decided exactly what the procedure is going to be,' Nigel declared reasonably, eyeing the man opposite. 'When are you leaving for the States?'

'Sunday after next,' he said. 'Pan American.'

'Then Sara can travel out any time that week.'

'No.' The tone was level enough but inflexible too. 'She travels with me.'

The older man's brows lifted a fraction. 'What difference does it make provided you're both available to complete any necessary formalities? In fact, strictly speaking, I doubt if your presence is going to be essential at all, if it comes to that. I've been taking advice. All Sara has to do is file. Provided you don't intend contesting it, the rest shouldn't be any problem.'

Sara's brows had drawn together. 'You've spoken with a lawyer?'

'An old friend who can be trusted to keep his own counsel.'

'But about *my* business.'

'It concerns me too,' he said mildly. 'At least, I thought it did.'

She was immediately penitent. 'Of course, I'm sorry. I'm not thinking very straight, that's all.'

'My fault,' drawled Dave. He left it there for a calculated moment, eyes mocking Sara's swift run of colour. 'I gave her a shock turning up without warning,' he tagged on. 'It was a last-minute invite— filling in for somebody else who couldn't make it.'

'It's all publicity, I suppose.' Whether Nigel was deceived was difficult to tell. 'Shall you be playing at all before going to the States?'

'Tomorrow,' Dave acknowledged, 'and the next night. Then there's the Open. I'm going to be pretty tied up the whole time.' He finished his coffee, glancing at his watch as he put down the cup. 'I'd better be making tracks if I'm going to get that train. The next one isn't till the early hours. Have you got a number I can ring for a taxi, Sara?'

'Side of the phone,' she said, trying to conceal her relief. 'Mini-cab.' She got up when he did, avoiding Nigel's eyes as she began gathering the cups and saucers. 'I'll just get these out of the way.'

The phone call had been made when she came back from the kitchen. 'Five minutes,' Dave advised. 'I'll go down and wait for it.' He nodded to the older man. 'I don't expect we'll be meeting again.'

'It's doubtful,' came the agreement. 'Good luck for the future.'

'You too.'

Sara accompanied him to the door. Emotionally, she felt a complete mess, wanting him to go yet not wanting it too. She could hardly find her voice, much less the cool command she needed. 'See you a week on Sunday,' she said, low-toned. 'And . . . thanks.'

'For what I did—or didn't do?' he asked satirically. 'Hope you think about what I said. You're not going to find what you're looking for in *that* direction.'

She resisted slamming the door in his wake, gathering herself before going back to face Nigel.

'Sorry about that,' she said, thinking she seemed to be doing little but apologise tonight. 'I couldn't get rid of him.'

'I understand.' He studied her, expression reflective. 'That obviously wasn't the reason you wanted to see me tonight.'

She had almost forgotten the other matter. It came back to her now full force. 'I had a phone call from a journalist friend this morning,' she said. 'We've been spotted together. So far I haven't been identfied, but that isn't to say I shan't be. I thought you should know.'

The sigh was heavy. 'I suppose it had to happen eventually, no matter how circumspect we were. What are they saying? No, don't answer that. I can guess.'

'The question is,' Sara said carefully, 'what we're going to do about it. If somebody is already taking an interest it isn't going to be long before they find out who I am. It won't hurt me, but that kind of publicity is hardly going to do you any good.'

He shrugged. 'It might create a bit of a stir, but it will soon be forgotten.'

'You know that's not true, not in your case. Discretion is supposed to be your stock-in-trade.'

It was a moment before he responded to that, the expression in his eyes difficult to assess. 'So what are you suggesting?' he asked at length.

'I think we have to let the whole thing fade out,' she said. 'Stop seeing each other for a few weeks. If I do have to stay on in Reno, all the better.' Her smile was wry. 'I'm talking sense, Nigel, we both know it.'

His own smile came slow and rueful. 'Sara, be honest with me. Be honest with yourself, if it comes to that. You're not sure any more, are you?'

'Of course I'm sure!' She said it with emphasis. 'Nothing's changed. I just . . .'

'You just need time to think, is that what you're going to say?' He shook his head. 'I'm not dense. I could feel the atmosphere in here as soon as I walked through that door tonight. It was like electricity between the two of you.' He paused, added softly, 'You're still in love with him, aren't you?'

'No!' The denial was jerked from her. 'I never did love him.'

'You mean you never allowed yourself time to overcome your differences. He could give you a great deal more than I ever could, Sara. Children, for one thing. Oh, I'm not saying I couldn't father a child, but at my age the patter of little feet doesn't hold the same appeal. And don't try telling me you don't want children, because I wouldn't believe it.'

'It isn't vital,' she said, 'it really isn't.' She made a gesture of appeal. 'Nigel . . .'

'I think we should both of us take a little time to think things over,' he said.

Her chest hurt. 'You already decided, didn't you? You don't want me any more.'

'I want you.' The emotion was there under the surface, but controlled. 'You're beautiful, intelligent, warm . . .' He broke off, inclining his head. 'That's by the way. The mistake I made was in ever believing I could make up all the missing years.'

Sara was still as he leaned forward to kiss her very gently on the lips, sensing the futility in further appeals. It was over. That much was already too clear. The doubts must have been there in his mind before any of this; he was probably grateful for the excuse to be rid of her. From somewhere she found the ability to dissemble.

'You're right, of course. It would probably never have worked out. I only hope it isn't too late to stop the gossip.'

'As you said, it will die a natural death.' He went to the door, looking back before passing through to say quietly, 'It isn't too late to start again, Sara, You're still married to the man.'

Only in name, she thought numbly as he carried on out. Dave might still want her body, but it was all he did want.

CHAPTER ELEVEN

SURROUNDED by mountains, and more than six thousand feet above sea level, Lake Tahoe offered scenic beauty in addition to its sophisticated gambling casinos. The latter were actually confined to a strip along the southern shore on the Nevada side of the stateline bisecting the lake. In happier circumstances, Sara would have preferred to stay on the less developed Californian side. The way things were, surroundings seemed of little importance.

Turning from the hotel window, she glanced at her watch. It was almost time for dinner, although she had never felt less like eating. Dave had said he would meet her downstairs. As before, they were occupying adjoining rooms, but this time the connecting doors remained closed and locked, symbolic of his attitude since they had met in the airport this morning. Whatever his thoughts and feelings, he wasn't revealing them.

Apart from a couple of phone calls, there had been no contact between them this past week and a half. He had made all the arrangements himself, refusing to accept any financial contribution on her part. The fact that it was no longer essential to try jumping the three-year limit had given her some sleepless nights, but she hadn't been able to bring herself to call it off. Pride again, she supposed. It had always been her downfall. Tomorrow she was going to find a lawyer and get the whole thing under way. It wouldn't be difficult; there was any number listed in the telephone directory. They even touted for business in the newspapers. Once Dave had left she would probably move into Reno itself for the time it took to finalise proceedings. In the meantime, there was a whole week to get through. It wasn't going to be easy.

Emerging from the elevator some minutes later, she found Dave signing an autograph for a girl who, from her dress, was employed by the complex. She was no more than nineteen or twenty, and straight off a chocolate-box cover to boot. Laughing, looking up flirtatiously into his eyes, she was openly inviting his interest. Sara waited until she had moved on before approaching him, her smile just a little stiff.

'Sorry I'm late, I couldn't get an elevator. At least you weren't lonely.'

'No.' His own smile was reminiscent. 'She was offering to show me the town later when she finishes work.'

'You should have taken her up on it. I'll be having an early night anyway.'

'We're invited to some kind of celebrity get-together right here in the hotel,' he returned, ignoring the comment. 'You wouldn't want to miss that, would you?'

Sara lifted her brows. 'We?'

'Myself and partner.'

'Then you could take your little friend.'

'I already told them I'd be bringing my wife,' he stated flatly. 'You could always amuse yourself spotting famous faces.'

It was a moment before she could find an answer. 'Isn't it rather ridiculous pretending to be a happily married couple, considering the reason I'm here at all?'

The shrug was negligent. 'We don't have to pretend anything. Amicable divorce is nothing new. You might even gain some advice on who to go through—unless you came ready armed with the name of a good lawyer?'

She shook her head. 'I understood there was no shortage.'

'Shouldn't imagine there is. It's big business out here.' He paused, studying her reflectively. 'You realise it isn't going to come cheap?'

'Of course.' Standing here amidst all the flashing lights and ringing bells, the hordes of people, she felt suddenly suffocated. 'Everything costs.'

'And with Rotherby champing at the bit, why should you worry?' he agreed. 'I'll pay my share.'

She said huskily, 'I never wanted a penny from you, Dave. I'm the one who instigated all this.'

His smile was crooked. 'An uncontested divorce means both partners have to be willing. I'll be gaining my freedom too, remember.'

'To marry again?'

'Maybe. One thing you can be sure of, next time it won't be any spur-of-the-moment idea.' He moved abruptly. 'Let's go and eat.'

The party was to publicise the opening of the hotel's new showroom—the biggest and most lavish, by all accounts, in the whole of Nevada. Stars of stage and screen abounded, but Sara could conjure little real interest. She felt listless and dull, as if she were coming down with something.

Jet-lag, she told herself, finding a corner where she could be alone for a few minutes. All she needed was sleep. Tomorrow she would be fine again.

'You look as bored with this as I am,' remarked a blond-haired young man who looked vaguely familiar, pausing by the potted palm she was using for semi-concealment. 'Feel like moving on somewhere?'

The smile which accompanied the invitation was devastating. Sara found herself smiling back. 'You don't believe in wasting time.'

'Life's too short,' he agreed. 'What say you?'

She snapped her fingers in sudden and triumphant recognition. 'I thought I knew your face! You're Christopher Leyton.'

'The same,' he acknowledged, sounding amused. 'Which of my movies have you seen?'

'I haven't actually seen any of them,' Sara confessed. 'I remember you from a magazine write-up last year. There was a full-page photograph.'

'Favourable, I hope.'

She laughed. 'Impressive! They were hailing you as the new Robert Redford.'

'I could act him off the set any day of the week,' came the derisive retort. 'English, aren't you?'

'How did you guess?'

'The accent,' he said, taking the question seriously. 'Why don't we get out of here?'

She shook her head, trying to look properly regretful. 'I'm with my husband.'

'Oh?' He turned to view the milling throng. 'Which one?'

'Over there,' she indicated, catching a glimpse as someone moved. 'Talking to the woman in green.'

'Isn't he world champion of something or other?' He gave her no chance to answer that one. 'Seems pretty wrapped up to me. Would he miss you?'

Probably not, she thought. If he noticed at all, he would assume she had gone to bed. Not a bad idea at that, the way she felt.

'It's almost six in the morning by our time,' she said, keeping her tone as light as his. 'We'll be leaving soon.'

His shrug suggested a philosophical acceptance. 'Hope he's worth it, honey!'

Sara watched him move away, aware that there were always plenty more fish in the sea for men like Christopher Leyton. He hadn't even bothered to ask her name. She could no longer see Dave when she looked back to the spot where he had been standing. There were too many people in between.

What exactly *was* he worth to her? she asked herself soberly. Did she love him enough to sink her pride and let him know it, or was she going to carry on through with this farce of a divorce? Because farce it was. It always had been. There had never really been a time when she had wanted it. Nigel had simply provided her with the excuse to go and see Dave, except he hadn't reacted the way she had planned in those inner recesses of her mind. He hadn't denied her what she had asked; he hadn't swept her up in a passionate embrace and vowed never to let her go again. That had been a fantasy of her own making. She was facing the truth—the real truth—for the first time, and it hurt.

Tonight might be her last chance to alter the direction in which their lives were leading, she acknowledged; the last chance to stop the roundabout she herself had set in motion. It was never too late to try again, wasn't that what they said? She could still stir Dave physically. That had to be a start.

The crowd began thinning as people moved on through to their reserved seats for the grand opening spectacular. When Dave did put in an appearance he was alone.

'If we're going in we'd better go now,' he said. 'It's due to start in a few minutes.'

'I was just getting round to throwing in the towel,' Sara confessed quite truthfully. 'No reason why you shouldn't see it though.'

'No reason at all,' he agreed, 'except that I've had enough too. We've both been on the go for almost twenty-four hours.'

It was impossible to tell from his expression what might be going on in his mind. Sara could only cling to the hope that he would make the first move, no matter what his motives. Once they were together she would find the words she needed. She had to find them. If she could have him back she wouldn't give a damn where or how they lived.

There were others in the elevator. Standing at Dave's side, feeling the brush of his jacket against her bare arm, she could scarcely contain her emotions. Three more floors and they would be there. She watched the numbers light up in rotation: ten—eleven—twelve. The doors opened and she stepped forward, thanking those who moved aside to allow her passage.

Dave was a step or two behind her going along the corridor, having held back to allow another couple priority. Her room number was lower than his, and therefore first in line. She was conscious of her fingers trembling as she inserted the key in the lock.

'It won't turn,' she said truthfully as he came level with her, glad of the excuse. 'It seems to be stuck.'

His fingers closed lightly over hers, turning the key in the opposite direction and pushing open the door. 'Clockwise here,' he said. 'You made the same mistake last time.'

'So I did.' She was vibrantly aware of his closeness, of the warmth of his breath on her temple. Her voice felt thick in her throat. 'It just goes to show how slow I am to learn.'

Just for a moment he seemed to hesitate, then someone opened a door up ahead and the moment was gone. 'You're not on your own,' he said quietly, and continued on along the corridor, leaving her to pass blindly through into the darkened room with a great empty gulf inside her.

She felt mercifully numb while she was preparing for bed. Only when it came to sliding between the smooth, fresh sheets did it come home to her how little real effort she had made. So far as Dave was concerned, she still planned on marrying another man. How would she feel if the positions were reversed? Waiting until the morning was no solution. She couldn't survive that long without knowing the worst. It had to be tonight.

Pulling on her wrap again, she resolutely crossed the room. The lock on her own side of the communicating doors turned noiselessly. Lifting a hand before courage deserted her altogether, Sara knocked softly on the featureless wood. She had to knock twice more before she heard movement on the other side.

Dave was wearing the hotel's own monogrammed bathrobe, his legs and feet bare beneath it. From the tousled look of his hair he had already been in bed. He just stood there looking at her, not helping at all.

I want to talk to you, Sara had meant to say, but she only got as far as the first two words before his lip started curling.

'Feeling the pinch already?'

'You didn't let me finish,' she said. 'Dave, I . . .'

'You don't have to lower yourself to beg,' he cut in again with irony. 'If you're that desperate I'm more than willing to oblige, Your room or mine?'

'Neither.' She hurt everywhere, but she had to go on. 'Dave, let me talk to you. Please!'

He studied her narrowly, eyes cold. 'Going to ask me to be best man at your wedding?'

'I'm not marrying Nigel.' She brought it out in a rush before he could say anything else, watching his expression undergo some indecipherable change. 'I should have told you before,' she added wretchedly. 'There's no need for all this now.'

It was a moment before he spoke. 'So why didn't you?'

It was her opportunity to be open with him, to tell him what was in her heart, but the words wouldn't come. 'I thought it was too late,' she said instead. 'It was only tonight when you started talking about how much it was going to cost that I realised how ridiculous it would be when it isn't even necessary any more.'

'You mean you're willing to wait for an English divorce?'

'I don't want a divorce.' There, she had said it. She watched for his reaction, but this time there was none. He just continued to look at her, as if she were a specimen under a microscope.

'Let me be sure about this,' he said when she had begun to think he wasn't going to make any comment at all. 'You're suggesting we give it another try?'

'Yes.' She was grateful that he'd come so quickly to the point. 'We never really gave it a chance the first time round.' She paused, then made an appealing little gesture. 'Do we have to stand here like this discussing it?'

Something flashed in his eyes. 'No, we don't. Not when there's a better place.'

He swung her up in his arms and carried her across to the bed she had already turned down, setting her back on her feet in order to slide the silky wrap from her shoulders. She quivered when he took the thin straps of her nightdress and drew them down over her arms, sliding her fingers into his hair as he bent to mouth each springing nipple; holding him to her in an ecstasy of sensation.

'That feels so good!' she groaned. 'Oh, Dave, you don't know how much I . . .'

He came up swiftly, surely, to find her mouth, smothering the words in a kiss that seared. His tongue parted her lips, its tip a delicate probe seeking union with her own, lighting a fire in the very centre of her body. Hands trembling, she opened his robe. He was naked beneath, his body so wonderfully firm and taut. She took her lips from his to press them instead to his chest, just below the hollow of his throat, tasting the salt on his skin beneath the coating of hair, running her tongue lightly down his breastbone as she sank slowly to her knees. Her fingers traced the remembered paths over flank and hip, finding each pulsing nerve, each sensitive crevice. It had been so long since she had known him like this. Last time had been too quick, too intense. She wanted to prolong every moment of this reunion, to recapture every last nuance of what they had been to each other. He made no move, giving her free rein, his only reaction the harsh rise and fall of his breathing, the faint trembling in his loins. He was velvet and steel, vibrant with life. She could never have enough of him.

He took her right there on the floor in the end, the thickness of the rug cushioning her against the hardness beneath. Limbs wrapped about him, Sara gave herself over to the wildness that was in her, moaning her need as he filled the emptiness inside her, answering each powerful stroke with eager hips. But it was Dave in control, making her wait for the fulfilment she craved, holding himself in check until her moans became pleas, until her whole body arched in frenzy beneath him, begging for release. When he finally let go it was as if the world itself had shattered into a million pieces.

The open fronts of the robe he was still wearing draped down over the two of them as they lay there, cocooning them in a warmth even the air-conditioning couldn't reach. Sara felt content to stay where she was for ever, regardless of the growing hardness of the floor at her back. She could feel Dave inside her still; a feeling she didn't want to lose. Whenever they were together like this there were no problems. no outside influences. They were one person.

'We'd better get up,' he said after a while. He sounded reluctant himself. 'We can't sleep on the floor.'

His cheek was close. Sara put her lips to it, feeling the slight roughness. Tomorrow when they woke his jawline would be shadowed, bristly to the touch. She would watch him shave the way she used to, delighting in the smooth sweep of the razor, the texture of the skin revealed. He never used an electric razor—at least he hadn't. In two years many things might have changed.

'I love you,' she whispered, giving way to emotion. 'I always have.'

'Sure you have.' He eased his weight from her, kneeling up to pull the robe about him. His mouth was slanted. 'Are we going to use your room or mine?'

'Does it matter?' She was sitting up herself now, arms clasping her raised knees. 'Dave, I mean it. I've been such a fool. I thought there were things more important than being with you.'

'And now you don't. Just like that?' He shook his head, the smile still curling his lip. 'Like you said in that note you left me, we made one mistake, don't let's compound it. What we've got isn't love. It's good, I'll grant you, but no more nor less than last time. If it wasn't enough then, it isn't going to be enough now.'

'Last time was two whole years ago,' she protested. 'We're different people—at least, I am.'

'I don't think so. You still want the same things. You go and marry your knight, sweetheart. He can give you most of them.'

'It's over,' she said desperately. 'I never really wanted to marry Nigel.'

'You mean you were using him?'

Her eyes dropped. 'In a way, yes, I suppose I was. He was my excuse for seeing you again—my face-saver, if you like. He guessed how I still felt about you that night you came to the flat.'

'And stood down like the gentleman he is?' The tone was derisive. 'Try again. If anybody did the ditching, you did. The poor devil was too far gone to see straight.'

'He told you that?'

'He didn't have to tell me. It was obvious the way he looked at you.'

'How would you know the way a man like Nigel Rotherby thinks and feels?' she flashed.

'Because on a certain level we're most of us of a mind.' Dave had got to his feet, hands thrust deep into the pockets of his robe as he stood over her. 'You affected him the same way you affect me. If it's really off he had a lucky escape, because it's doubtful if you'd have stuck it for long. You couldn't bear anything that wasn't satisfying all your needs.'

'You might have been right once,' Sara acknowledged, 'but not now. Not where you're concerned.' Her voice shook a little. 'If there's one thing I've discovered, it's that people matter more than places and things. I'll live wherever you live, any place you want—and that's more than you ever offered to do for me.'

'Probably because I didn't see myself making the sacrifice, any more than I see you doing it now. We're both selfish people in our own way. He paused, regard hard and unyielding, and added brusquely, 'You know what my initial reaction was when I got back home and found that note of yours waiting for me? Relief. I actually felt relieved! You weren't the only one who knew we'd made a bad mistake. The only thing I'd been able to hope for was that we'd eventually come to terms.'

Sara swallowed painfully on the lump in her throat. 'You said initially. What about afterwards, when you'd had time to think about it?'

'Oh, I missed you right enough. What man wouldn't?'

'But not enough to come after me.'

A muscle jerked suddenly in the side of his jaw. 'I had my pride too. You did the leaving.'

'And there were always those willing to compensate for what you were missing, I suppose!'

'Not right away. I was off women altogether for a few months.' His smile lacked humour. 'I was off my game too, if it comes to that. I got knocked out of the following year's championship in the first round.'

'And you blamed me for that?'

'Partly. Still, I got over it.' He moved to pick up her wrap from the floor where he had dropped it, holding it out for her. 'Put this on before you get a chill from the air-conditioning.'

She was chilled already, but in her heart not her body. Yet what other attitude might she have anticipated when it came right down to it? Dave hadn't loved her then and he didn't love her now. Why should he take her back? Sex wasn't enough to keep a marriage going; they had already proved that.

'I need a shower,' she said, standing up to slide her arms into the wrap and belt it about her.

'Me too.'

He didn't suggest they took it together, moving off into his own room, though leaving both doors ajar. Standing under the warm, gushing water. Sara tried to think about what she was going to do now. Staying here was out of the question. To see Dave every day knowing it was all finished would be more than she could bear. Yet the thought of returning home held even less attraction. There was nothing there that she cared about. Not any more. Perhaps she should travel for a while—see something of the States while she was over here. She was twenty-five years old. Life had to go on. They would get the divorce next year, regardless. There would be other men: love didn't happen just once. One day she would meet someone who would make her forget all about Dave Lyness.

The sight of him lying in her bed when she went through from the bathroom made her heart leap in sudden hope, but he soon deflated her again.

'There's no reason why we shouldn't enjoy what we have got,' he declared as she hesitated in the doorway. 'What say you?'

It was storing up more pain for herself, she knew, yet she couldn't find the strength to turn down the offer. Tomorrow she would make arrangements to leave; for tonight there was no denying the temptation. She wanted to waken once more in Dave's arms, to kiss his lips and feel his body harden against her, to know that early-morning vitality which sprang from a good night's sleep. Just this one last night, no more. Was it so much to give away?

It didn't stop at that, of course. Each and every day was to be her last, only she somehow never got round to packing her things and checking out. The mornings were long and lazy, the afternoons spent sunbathing round the pool. In the evenings, after Dave was finished for the day, they might take in a show, or visit one of the casinos, returning to the hotel in the early hours to make love with undiminished fervour. The future wasn't mentioned, yet Sara doubted if Dave had in any way changed his mind. If she was still here by the weekend, she would have two choices. Either she flew back to England on the same plane and parted at the airport, or she took up the alternative plan and set off on her own somewhere. The latter might be easier in the long run in that it provided a swifter, cleaner break. Ten or more hours on a plane thinking about it would hardly make for a pleasant journey.

It was Dave's suggestion that they take out a boat on his free afternoon and picnic in Emerald Bay along the coastline. They could climb up to Eagle Falls, which the guide book said had crystal clear pools for swimming. Sara didn't care what they did provided they did it together, but she refrained from telling him that in case he misconstrued it as another plea for a reconciliation. It wouldn't be any use: he had made that plain enough. He might regret her passing when the time came, but he would get over it. So would she—eventually.

They hired a fast, two-seater speedboat, and took a packed lunch from the hotel. The lake was so vast it was almost like being at sea. Twenty-two miles long and twelve wide. it was also over fifteen hundred feet deep, Sara had read. It made her a little nervous, especially with the wind roughening the surface as they got further away from the land, causing the boat to bounce from wave to wave. She wasn't such a very good swimmer.

Dave himself seemed unperturbed by the motion. He simply coaxed more speed from the engine, lifting the bows right out of the water as they raced towards the distant landline. With her hair peeled back from her face and her eyes watering despite the protecting windshield, Sara could only hang on and hope for the best. Not for anything was she going to ruin his enjoyment by asking him to slow down.

Emerald Bay lived up to its name, a near-land-locked jewel of a place. Dave slowed the boat as they passed between the points, on the lookout for the speed patrol they had been warned about back at the jetty. Ponderosa pine grew right down to the water's edge, stretching back into the mountains beyond. All was peace and tranquillity beneath a cloudless blue sky.

'Could be a thousand miles from anywhere,' he commented with satisfaction, bringing them in to a narrow crescent of beach. 'Do you want to make that trip up to Eagle Falls, or shall we stay and eat here?'

'Here,' Sara decided. 'It's too far in this heat. Anyway, we shouldn't leave the boat.'

'I doubt if anybody would spot it down by the side of these rocks, but you're probably right. You take the food while I make fast.'

Sara kicked off her sandals and slid over the side, splashing through the shallows to the warm sand. The only way they could be seen was from the water itself, and at present there was no other craft in sight. They had the whole golden afternoon to themselves.

And after it, what? came the thought. All she was doing was prolonging the inevitable. Come Sunday Dave would be leaving, with her or without her. He didn't care what happened to her. He was simply taking advantage of her own weakness, even today he had brought her here with purpose.

If he noted her sudden change of mood he made no comment. Nor did he attempt to come near her when they'd finished eating, settling himself back comfortably against a rock with his hands locked behind his head and eyes closed.

'That wine packed a punch,' he murmured lazily. 'Either that, or I'm getting old. Wake me in an hour.'

Sara waited until his breathing had evened out before allowing herself to glance his way. Like her, he was wearing shorts and tee-shirt with bathing things underneath. His legs were strong and brown beneath the fine coating of hair, the thigh muscles clearly defined. She could visualise every inch of that lean-hipped, vital body, but it gave her no rights. There had been other women in his life already, and there would certainly be more. The thought of someone else living with him, perhaps bearing his child one day, ripped her apart. She could have had it all.

Whether from the wine she had drunk or simply the sun, her head was pounding. The water looked so cool, so inviting, so calm here within the protection of the bay. Some hundred yards or so out rose a tiny islet. She could reach that easily. Better than sitting here going over and over the same stony ground.

Quietly, she slipped out of her shorts and shirt, leaving them folded neatly on the sand. Warmed by the sun, the shallower water felt delicious, yet within a few yards it became so cold it began taking her breath. Melted snow, of course, from the mountains. The higher peaks still carried white crowns. Tantalisingly, the islet seemed to retreat as she swam slowly towards it. In the end she turned to go back, shocked to see how far away the shore looked.

Her limbs felt heavy and lifeless, her heartbeats sluggish. When she slipped below the surface the first time it was an effort to even raise her head. She could see Dave stretched out where she had left him on the sand, but when she tried to shout she took in water and went under again. She was going to drown, came the hazy thought. A perfectly calm sea, and she was going to drown. Oddly enough there was no panic, no desire to struggle. The water was full of dancing silver lights, drawing her downwards, downwards, until the pain in her chest exploded and she knew no more.

She recovered consciousness to find herself face down on the sand, her body racked by a terrible retching as Dave forced water from her lungs. He desisted as soon as he saw her move her head, sitting back on his heels with the breath whistling between his teeth.

'Thank God!' he said. 'I thought I was too late.' His voice was rough, close to anger. 'What the hell made you go in there on your own right after a meal!'

'It wasn't cramp,' she murmured, trying to remember. 'It was just so cold, and I was so hot.' She hiccupped more water and began suddenly to shiver, pushing her balled fist against her lips with a strangled sob. 'Hold me,' she begged. 'Don't say any more, just hold me.'

He gathered her close, turning her into his shoulder, laying his cheek against her wet hair. She could feel his warmth seeping into her, hear his heartbeats like thunder in her ears.

'I thought I'd lost you,' he said thickly. 'You'd gone under before I could reach you. I had to dive twice before I found you. God, I've been a fool! I could no more walk away from you than fly! I love you, do you hear me? I love you, I want you, and I'm never going to let you leave me again, so don't even try!'

She was dreaming, Sara thought mistily. Either that or she was dead and this was heaven. 'I won't,' she promised, leaving the question in the air for the moment. 'I really won't. Dave, I . . .'

He silenced her with a kiss, cherishing her mouth the way she had yearned for. 'We'll have all the time in the world for talking later,' he said. 'Right now we're going to get you to a doctor.'

'I'm all right,' she assured him. 'I'm more than all right.' She put up a hand to his cheek, smile only a little shaky. 'If I had to go through it all over again it would still be worth it. We've wasted so much time, Dave. Two whole years.'

A shadow passed across his face. 'Nothing's really changed, though, has it? I can't give it up, Sara. Not yet a while anyway. I know how you hate the game, but . . .'

'I don't hate it,' she denied, 'I never hated it. I only resented it because it took you away from me.'

'It still will.'

'So I'll come with you. Not all the time, perhaps, but some of it.' Her strength was coming back, the shakiness fading. She pressed her lips to his bare wet chest. 'I'll be busy making a home for us—a real home. I fancy a cottage in the country, with a nice big garden for the children to play in.'

He was smiling, if not yet quite convinced. 'You're getting a bit far ahead, aren't you?'

'Perhaps not,' she said. 'You see, I dropped off the pill this last couple of years, not having found anyone else I wanted to go to bed with, and you didn't give me much time to think about it that night you came to the flat. There's a very fair chance I might already be pregnant, especially considering I haven't taken any precautions this week either.' She added frankly, 'I may have been preparing the ground for a spot of emotional blackmail. The way my mind's been working lately I wouldn't be sure. The only thing I am sure of is how I feel about you. I've been going through hell these last few days.'

'I was a swine,' Dave admitted. 'I wanted to make you hurt. If it's any consolation, it didn't give me the satisfaction I imagined it would, only I couldn't seem to get round to telling you I'd changed my mind.' He kissed her again, then rose resolutely to his feet, drawing her along with him. 'We're going back before I get side-tracked. First a doctor, then a good long rest. It was too close to take any chances.'

It had been close all right, she thought as he went to untie the boat. If she hadn't almost drowned herself they might never have reached this point. Three more days and they would be going home. It wasn't going to be all plain sailing, but this time they were going to make it. She had never been surer of anything in her life.

Harlequin Presents

Coming Next Month

ATTRACTIVE, SPACE SAVING BOOK RACK

Display your most prized novels on this handsome and sturdy book rack. The hand-rubbed walnut finish will blend into your library decor with quiet elegance, providing a practical organizer for your favorite hard-or soft-covered books.

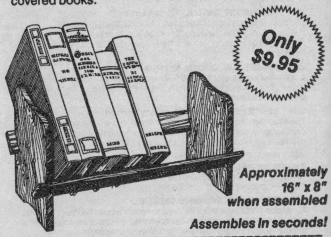

Only
$9.95

Approximately
16" x 8"
when assembled

Assembles in seconds!

To order, rush your name, address and zip code, along with a check or money order for $10.70* ($9.95 plus 75¢ postage and handling) payable to *Harlequin Reader Service*:

Harlequin Reader Service
Book Rack Offer
901 Fuhrmann Blvd.
P.O. Box 1325
Buffalo, NY 14269-1325

Offer not available in Canada.

*New York residents add appropriate sales tax.

BKR-1R

Can you keep a secret?

You can keep this one plus 4 free novels

Here's how to get this special offer from Harlequin!

As simple as 1...2...3!

1. Each month, save one Treasury Edition coupon from your favorite Romance or Presents novel.
2. In four months you'll have saved four Treasury Edition coupons (only one coupon per month allowed).
3. Then all you have to do is fill out and return the order form provided, along with the four Treasury Edition coupons required and $2.95 for postage and handling.

Mail to: Harlequin Reader Service

In the U.S.A.	In Canada
901 Fuhrmann Blvd.	P.O. Box 609
P.O. Box 1397	Fort Erie, Ontario
Buffalo, NY 14240	L2A 9Z9

BN-Dec-2

Please send me my Special copy of the Betty Neels Treasury Edition. I have enclosed the four Treasury Edition coupons required and $2.95 for postage and handling along with this order form. (Please Print)

NAME_____

ADDRESS_____

CITY_____

STATE/PROV._____ ZIP/POSTAL CODE_____

SIGNATURE_____

This offer is limited to one order per household.

SUPPLIES LIMITED

This special Betty Neels offer expires February 28, 1987.

Janet Dailey

Americana

Don't miss a single title from this great collection. The first eight titles
have already been published. Complete and mail this coupon today to
order books you may have missed.

Harlequin Reader Service

In U.S.A.
901 Fuhrmann Blvd.
P.O. Box 1397
Buffalo, N.Y. 14140

In Canada
P.O. Box 2800
Postal Station A
5170 Yonge Street
Willowdale, Ont. M2N 6J3

Please send me the following titles from the Janet Dailey Americana
Collection. I am enclosing a check or money order for $2.75 for each
book ordered, plus 75¢ for postage and handling.

_____	ALABAMA	Dangerous Masquerade
_____	ALASKA	Northern Magic
_____	ARIZONA	Sonora Sundown
_____	ARKANSAS	Valley of the Vapours
_____	CALIFORNIA	Fire and Ice
_____	COLORADO	After the Storm
_____	CONNECTICUT	Difficult Decision
_____	DELAWARE	The Matchmakers

Number of titles checked @ $2.75 each = $_____

N.Y. RESIDENTS ADD
    APPROPRIATE SALES TAX $_____

Postage and Handling $____.75____

                              TOTAL $_____

I enclose _____

(Please send check or money order. We cannot be responsible for cash
sent through the mail.)

PLEASE PRINT

NAME _____

ADDRESS _____

CITY _____

STATE/PROV. _____

BLJD-A-1